59055

Is this any way to treat a guest?

"Cleveland!" Val said with a frown. "Behave yourself! Is that any way to treat a guest?"

"Raaoow!" said Cleveland. His ears were flattened to his head, and every hair on his body was standing on end, making him look even bigger than he actually was.

Andy stood up on his hind legs with his front paws on the top rail of the crib and began to bark. Hearing all the noise, the chickens and the duck began to cluck and quack. Val clapped her hands over her ears. "Quiet down, you guys!" she yelled.

Andy's barking turned into excited whines as Val came over and patted his spiky head. Cleveland lashed his tail, mumbling cat curses to himself.

"I'm ashamed of you, Cleveland," Val said sternly. "You act like you've never seen a dog before."

Siskiyou County
School Library

Look for these and other books in the Animal Inn series from Apple Paperbacks:

#1 *Pets Are for Keeps*
#2 *A Kid's Best Friend*
#3 *Monkey Business*
#4 *Scaredy Cat*
#5 *Adopt-A-Pet*
#6 *All the Way Home*
#7 *The Pet Makeover*
#8 *Petnapped!*
#9 *One Dog Too Many*

ANIMAL INN

ONE DOG TOO MANY

Virginia Vail

AN
APPLE
PAPERBACK

Siskiyou County
School Library

SCHOLASTIC INC.
New York Toronto London Auckland Sydney

No part of this publication may be reproduced in whole or in part, or stored in a retrieval system, or transmitted in any form or by any means, electronic, mechanical, photocopying, recording, or otherwise, without written permission of the publisher. For information regarding permission, write to Scholastic Inc., 730 Broadway, New York, NY 10003.

ISBN 0-590-42800-4

Copyright © 1990 by Cloverdale Press and Jane Thornton. All rights reserved. Published by Scholastic Inc. APPLE PAPERBACKS is a registered trademark of Scholastic Inc.

12 11 10 9 8 7 6 5 4 3 2 0 1 2 3 4 5/9

Printed in the U.S.A.

First Scholastic printing, August 1990 40

For Melody, Kayla, Chrissy, Michael, Nicole, Katy, Meghan, Rebekah, and all the other fans of **ANIMAL INN** who have written such wonderful letters to me.

Chapter 1

Valentine Taylor was running as fast as she could. As she touched second base and headed for third, the cheers of her teammates rang in her ears. "Way to go, Taylor!" Sarah Jones yelled. Sarah was the best hitter on the girls' softball team of Hamilton Junior High, but this time it wasn't a real game where every point counted. This was just a game with Val and a few of her friends. All that mattered was having *fun*.

Val skidded into third base and glanced into the outfield. She saw her best friend, Jill Dearborne, staring helplessly down at the ball in her hand. Jill wasn't very athletic.

"What do I do now?" she yelled.

"*Throw* it! *Throw* it!" screamed the girls on Jill's team.

"*Where?*" Jill screamed back.

Before she could receive further instructions, Val started running again. By the time Jill had figured out that she was supposed to throw the ball to the catcher behind home plate, Val's triple had turned into a home run.

"We won!" Sarah cried, slapping Val on the back. "Hit like that when the season begins in the spring, and the Raiders will be area champs!"

Brushing strands of chestnut-brown hair out of her sweaty face, Val grinned. "I don't know about that," she said. "In a real game, the outfielder will probably know what to do with the ball." She grinned at Jill, who had just trotted off the field along with the other members of the opposing team. Jill's face was flushed and her short blonde hair was standing on end.

Scowling, Jill said, "Some friend you are, Val Taylor! You know I'm not a hotshot athlete like you. I only agreed to play this dumb game because you guys couldn't scrape together enough people for two teams!"

"Hey, Jill, you did real good — considering," Sarah said. She was about to slap Jill on the back, too, but Jill quickly stepped aside.

"Thanks, Sarah," she said. "But the next time you jocks decide to play ball after school, count me out!"

As the girls gathered up their belongings and began to leave the field, Val slung her backpack over her shoulder and held out Jill's. "Want to come over to my house for some lemonade?" she asked her friend. "I don't know about you, but I could drink about a gallon right now."

"Me, too." Jill smiled. Val knew she wasn't really angry. "I'd love to, but I told my mom I'd meet her at four-thirty at her office." Mrs. Dearborne was an interior decorator, the only one in Essex, Pennsylvania. "She's redoing my room, and she wants me to pick out the wallpaper and stuff. Call me tonight, okay? We can talk about our English assignment for tomorrow." She sighed. "I can't *believe* Mr. Steele gave us homework on the very first day of school!"

Val shrugged. "That's the way he is. And he's not the only one. It's like all the teachers just couldn't wait till summer vacation was over so they could start loading it on."

The two girls went over to their bikes that were leaning against the chain fence surrounding the field.

"I know exactly what my essay's going to be about — the petnapping!" Val said.

In August, she and her friend Toby had helped the sheriff find out who was stealing people's pets. They had even gotten their names in the *Essex Gazette*.

Jill mounted her bicycle. "Great. But what am

I supposed to write about my summer vacation? I didn't do anything interesting at all."

"You did too," Val said. "Your folks took you to Cape Cod for two whole weeks. You could write about that."

"Yeah, I guess." Jill began pedaling off. "Talk to you tonight — 'bye!"

Most of the other girls had already left, so Val got onto her bike and headed for home. She was about to turn onto Market Street when she realized that it was only four-fifteen. If she took a short cut down Codorus Avenue, she could pick up York Road and get to Animal Inn, her father's veterinary clinic, in about fifteen minutes. That would give her enough time to ride her horse, The Gray Ghost, before the clinic closed for the day. Then she could get a ride home with Doc.

The Ghost lived in a big white barn where Doc treated farm animals that were sick or injured. As much as she loved her horse, Val was always so busy that it was hard to spend as much time with him as she wanted. Today, she and The Ghost could have a nice ramble down the country lanes behind Animal Inn, but only if she hurried.

Codorus Avenue was not very well paved. There were lots of potholes, so Val had to pedal very slowly. It was when she was passing the fence around the highway department storage area that she heard a cry for help.

At first, she thought she was hearing things, but then she heard it again.

"Help! Help!" It was a man's voice.

As Val pulled over to the curb, she noticed that one of the big gates in the fence was open. Getting off her bike, she wheeled it to the opening and peered inside.

She couldn't see much because there were a lot of big highway department trucks blocking her view, so she took a few steps inside.

"*Help!*" the man yelled again.

"Where are you?" Val yelled back.

"Over here — by the basin!"

Basin? What basin? Val wondered. But she dropped the bike and started running in the direction of his voice. Dodging between two tar-smeared trucks, she found herself in an open area near a huge metal garage. Next to the garage she saw a man bending over some kind of pit. The man saw her, too, and waved frantically with one tarry hand. The other hand was holding onto something in the pit.

"Over here," he shouted, and Val raced to his side. The man had thinning gray hair, and his khaki pants and shirt were covered with tar. He looked up at her and groaned. "Oh no. You're just a kid!"

"What's wrong?" Val asked — and then she looked down. What she saw made her gasp. There was a dog floundering in the thick, black tar in the pit. The man was holding its head up out of the mess so it could breathe, but even the dog's head was so completely plastered with tar that Val couldn't tell what kind of dog it was.

Immediately she reached out and plunged her arms into the sticky, black goo, grabbing the animal around the chest.

"*Pull!*" she shouted. "Pull on his collar! I'll help you get him out!"

The man pulled, but the terrified dog snapped at him and he almost let go of the collar.

"Keep pulling!" Val cried, struggling to drag the animal to safety.

"What if he's got rabies?" the man said. "If he bites me, I could get rabies, too!" He was a very small man, Val noticed. He didn't look very strong.

"He won't bite you if you keep your hand *behind* his head," Val said between clenched teeth. "Pull!"

A moment later, the two of them dragged the dog out of the pit and plopped it on the ground. The animal just lay there, panting and whining. Every single inch of its body was covered with tar, but it was alive.

"We did it!" Val gasped. She was covered with

tar, too, from her chest to the toes of her sneakers. So was the man in the khaki uniform.

"Geez!" The man stared down at the heaving black blob at their feet. "I've been a security guard for Highways for more'n seven years, and I never seen anything like this!" He looked up at Val. "Thanks, kid. Good thing you came along. Strong, ain't 'cha?"

But Val was too concerned about the animal to pay any attention to what he said. She kneeled down next to the dog and looked into its eyes. They were big and brown and very scared.

"We have to take him to Animal Inn," she said. "My father will know what to do for him."

The security guard stared at her. "Animal Inn? That's the vet place, ain't it? The one on Orchard Lane? Is Doc Taylor your dad?"

"He sure is. I'm Valentine Taylor." She stood up. "Can somebody take the dog and me there right away?"

The man scratched his head, getting tar on his hair. "I dunno. I can't, that's for sure. I have to stay on duty till the night man relieves me, and he don't show up till six o'clock. And there's nobody else around."

"This is an *emergency*!" Val cried.

Looking down at the dog, the guard nodded.

"Guess you're right, kid — what did you say your name was?"

"Valentine, Val for short. *Please*, Mister . . ."

"Hoffman. Delbert Hoffman."

Val was practically jumping up and down with impatience. "Mr. Hoffman, there has to be a phone here somewhere. Tell me where it is and I'll call my father. If we don't get this dog to Animal Inn, he could *die*!"

"No need to do that," said Mr. Hoffman. "I got a walkie-talkie right here on my belt. All I have to do is contact the cops and they'll be here before you can say Jack Robinson."

Controlling herself with great effort, Val said, "Then would you please *do it*?"

"I *am* doing it," he said, unhitching the walkie-talkie. "Hey, Chuck, do you read me? This here's Del over at Highways. We got a problem — some dog fell into the tar basin and we gotta get him to the vet real fast. Send the car, okay?"

There was a crackle of static and a series of squawks that Val couldn't understand, but apparently Mr. Hoffman could. "I don't *know* how the durned dog got in!" he said. "What do you care? Just send the car — and make it snappy, or the dog's a goner. Over and out."

"We have to wrap him in something so he

doesn't mess up the police car," Val said.

"There're some old newspapers in the garage. I'll get 'em. You stay here, Valerie — be right back." Mr. Hoffman hurried off, and Val bent down to the quivering black blob at her feet.

"Don't worry," she said. "You're going to be all right, honest. I don't know if Dad's ever had a case like this, but that doesn't matter. He knows everything about animals and he'll take good care of you."

She reached out to pat him, and her tarry hand stuck to the dog's tarry fur. For a moment, Val was afraid she'd be permanently glued to it because the cool September breeze was making the tar even thicker than it already was. But she was able to pull her hand away just as Mr. Hoffman came trotting back with an armful of newspapers.

"Here you go, Veronica," he said. Looking at her, he grinned. "Maybe you better wrap yourself up, too — you're almost as messy as that there dog!"

A moment later, Val heard a siren. Essex's only police car was on its way. She ran to the open gate, waving and shouting, "In here! The dog's in here!"

With lights flashing and siren hooting, the blue-and-white car lurched into the enclosure and screeched to a stop. A few minutes later Val and Mr. Hoffman spread papers over the backseat and put the terrified animal in. Val climbed in beside it. As the police car sped away, she leaned out the window and called, " 'Bye, Mr. Hoffman! I'll let you know what happens!"

"You do that, Victoria," Mr. Hoffman called back.

Hardly more than five minutes later, the police car turned into Orchard Lane.

"Would you drop me in the parking lot in front of the Small Animal Clinic?" Val said to the police officer. "Then please take the dog to that white barn — I'll bring my dad over right away!"

She leaped out and raced into Animal Inn. Because it was late in the day, there were only a few animals and their owners waiting to see Doc Taylor, but all of them had heard the siren. The dogs were barking and the cats were yowling. Their owners bombarded Val with questions as she ran to the desk where Pat Dempwolf, Doc's receptionist, was sitting. But Val didn't have time to answer them.

"I have to see Dad right away!" she told Pat. "Where is he?"

Pat was so astonished by the sight of Val all covered with tar that she dropped several stitches in the sweater she was knitting for her granddaughter

Tiffany. "He's in the second treatment room. Vallie, what happened to you?"

"Tell you later!"

Val dashed out of the waiting room and flung open the door to the treatment room where her father was just finishing his examination of a very pregnant cat. "Butterball's going to be just fine," he was saying to the anxious woman who was hovering over the cat. When he saw Val, he stared at her. "Vallie, what on earth. . . ?"

"Dad, there's an emergency!" Val cried. "You have to come with me right away!"

Doc picked up the cat and handed her to her owner. "Here you go, Miss Ryder. Sorry, but I have to run — I'm sure you understand."

Clutching her cat, Miss Ryder scurried out, and Doc began scrubbing his hands in the little sink.

"Dad, *please* hurry!" Val wailed. "There's this dog . . . the police . . . oh, *hurry*!"

"Calm down, honey," Doc said. "I'm coming as fast as I can. Did you say the police? Where is this dog? And how come you look like you fell into a tar pit?"

"Because I did, almost." Val ripped off a paper towel and thrust it at him. "Mr. Hoffman did, too. He called the police and they picked up the dog and me. He's by the barn all covered with tar, and . . ."

"Who's by the barn? Mr. Hoffman? What about the dog?" Doc asked, thoroughly confused.

"The *dog's* by the barn," Val cried, grabbing her father's hand and pulling him after her as she ran out the door. "He's the one who really fell into the tar at that highway department place over on Codorus Avenue. Mr. Hoffman and I got him out, but he's in pretty bad shape. You have to help him, Dad, or I'm afraid he's going to die!"

Chapter 2

As Val and Doc rushed toward the Large Animal Clinic, they saw Toby Curran looking in the back window of the police car. Toby was fourteen, a year older than Val, and he also worked for Doc part-time. He turned around when he heard their footsteps pounding on the gravel drive.

"You're not gonna *believe* this dog!" he said to Doc. "If you didn't know it was a dog, you wouldn't know *what* it was!"

"That's for sure," said the officer behind the wheel. "Bet you never had a patient like this before, Doc Taylor."

Doc glanced into the backseat. "You know something, Officer Zarfoss? You are absolutely right." He rubbed his short, graying beard. "Toby, go get some rags, and one of those horse blankets we keep in the storage room — an *old* blanket. We'll wrap the animal in it so we can get him out of the car without making a bigger mess than there is already. Vallie, there's some kerosene in the shed out back," he said as Toby dashed into the barn. "Bring it here right away."

"Kerosene?" Val echoed. "But why . . ."

"Just do as I say, honey," Doc said, and Val sprinted off. When she came back lugging the can of kerosene, Doc and Toby had already placed the dog on the ground. It was standing on the tarry blanket, head hanging, and quivering all over.

"Oh, my goodness!" Donna Hartman, who ran Animal Inn's new grooming salon, came over and joined them as fast as she could, which wasn't very fast since she was almost eight months pregnant. "The poor thing!" she gasped. "What happened to it — and you, too, Val?"

Quickly, Val told her how she and Mr. Hoffman had rescued the dog. Then she turned to her father. "Dad, will all that gunk make him terribly sick?" she asked anxiously. "Could it kill him?"

Doc shook his head. "I very much doubt it, unless he swallowed a lot of tar before you got him out." He knelt beside the dog and gently raised its head and opened its jaws, peering into its mouth. "It doesn't look as if he's swallowed any at all," he said, and Val breathed a sigh of relief. Doc wiped his hands on a corner of the blanket and stood up. "But the sooner we get started cleaning him up, the better."

Officer Zarfoss leaned out the window of the police car. "Hey, Donna, that oughta be right up your alley. Cleaning up animals is your specialty, right?"

Laughing, Donna said, "I'm afraid it's too big a job for me. I wouldn't get done till the baby's born, and he or she isn't due for another six weeks!"

"Well, I guess it's up to you and these kids then," the policeman said to Doc. "Good luck!"

He started the engine, and Doc said, "Thanks for your help, Officer Zarfoss."

"Yes, thanks so much," Val added. "I never could have brought him here on my bike — my bike!" she exclaimed. "I forgot all about it! It's still at the highway place."

"Don't worry about it, honey," Doc said as the police car drove away. "We can get the bike later. Right now, the important thing is getting to work on this poor animal."

"And I'd better get back to work, too," Donna said. "I've got a poodle inside waiting for a manicure. Want me to tell Pat to reschedule the rest of your appointments, Doc?"

Doc nodded. "Good idea. But if any of those animals need immediate attention, ask her to let me know, okay?"

"Will do." Before she went back inside, Donna

looked down at the dog. "When you get all that stuff off, his fur's going to be in terrible shape. His skin will probably be really irritated, too. I have all kinds of shampoos and conditioners and moisturizers. You bring the poor thing to me and I'll give him the full treatment." She winked at Doc. "No charge, of course!"

Doc smiled. "Thanks, Donna. We'll definitely take you up on that offer."

Donna walked off, and Val said, "Dad, what do we do first?"

"Yeah, Doc — if you show Val and me what to do, I bet we can have this guy clean as a whistle in no time," Toby said.

"I wouldn't count on it," Doc told him. "It's not going to take six weeks, but it's not going to be a speedy job, either. And it's going to be a very messy one. How's your mother going to feel about you coming home all covered with tar?"

Toby shrugged. "No problem. These jeans are about shot anyway, and this shirt's had it, too. But I guess I better call and tell her I'm going to be late."

"Would you call our house, too, Toby?" Val asked. "We don't want Mrs. Racer to worry about us." Mrs. Racer was the Taylors' Mennonite housekeeper, and she also kept an eye on Val's younger brother and sister, Teddy and Erin, when neither Val nor Doc were around.

While Toby made his phone calls, Doc told Val, "Soak two of those rags with kerosene, Vallie, and we'll get started. Kerosene is a powerful solvent. If anything can break up this tar, it will. Too bad this fellow has such long hair."

Together they began scrubbing the patient animal's fur. He seemed to know that they were trying to help him and stood very still. Doc concentrated on the dog's face and ears, being very careful not to get any kerosene in his eyes. Val began at the other end, and soon discovered that her father was right — getting the tar off was going to take a very long time.

"Are there any tags on his collar, Dad?" she asked. "I didn't think to look before. He must belong to somebody, and his owner's going to start wondering where he is."

"I just checked," Doc said, dropping the collar on the ground. "No tags. But the *Gazette* will probably run an item about him in tomorrow's paper in the Police Blotter section. If anybody's missing a dog, they'll be sure to check there."

Toby came back and was assigned the animal's midsection. "Boy, does this stuff stink!" he muttered, scowling at the can of kerosene.

"That's one of the reasons we're working outside," Doc said. "We don't want to fill the barn with fumes. We also don't want to soak the floorboards with kerosene because of the risk of fire. Good thing it's a warm, sunny day."

"Give me another rag," Val sighed. "This one's putting more tar back on him than it's taking off, and I haven't even finished his tail yet!"

An hour later, Pat and Donna had gone home and Animal Inn's night man, Mike Strickler, had come on duty. Almost all the kerosene was used up and most of the rags were stiff with tar, but the dog didn't look much different. Toby, Doc, and Val, however, were black from head to toe. Val was beginning to get discouraged, Toby was getting hungry, the dog was starting to whimper, and even Doc's usual cheerfulness was fading.

Val got stiffly to her feet, rubbing her aching back. "At this rate, we're going to be here all night," she groaned.

"I didn't tell my mom I'd be *this* late," Toby said, peering at his watch through the film of tar that covered it. "It's almost half past six."

"You go home, Toby," Doc said wearily. "And thanks for all your hard work. Believe me, I appreciate it."

Toby hesitated for a moment, then said, "Okay. See you tomorrow, I guess. Uh . . . what're you gonna do with him tonight? I mean, where's he gonna sleep?"

"Beats me," Doc confessed. "But we'll think of something. 'Bye Toby, and thanks again."

Toby trudged off to get his bike, and Val squatted down next to the dog, patting its sticky head. "I'm sorry, fella," she said. "I guess you're still feeling pretty miserable, huh?" She looked up at her father. "Isn't there something else we can do for him, Dad? It doesn't look like we're ever going to be able to get all this stuff off." The dog licked her face, and she smiled. "At least he doesn't hold it against us."

"He certainly has a remarkable disposition," Doc said. "We owe it to him to keep doing the best we can. I think it's time we tried more drastic measures."

"Like what?" Val asked.

"Well, it's obvious that we're never going to get his fur clean this way — there's too much of it and it's too long. Vallie, I want you to go into Donna's beauty parlor and get a pair of scissors — make that *two* pairs. We're going to give our patient a haircut. It won't be as professional a job as Donna would do, but in this case, beauty isn't the object."

Val nodded. "You're right, Dad. But we'll probably have to buy Donna some new scissors afterward."

She ran back to Animal Inn and returned a few minutes later with several pairs of sharp, bright scissors. Once again, Val started at the dog's tail while Doc worked on its head, snipping away the matted fur. When they finally met in the middle, the animal was knee-deep in clumps of tarry fur. What remained on its body stood up in stiff black tufts, though Val could see a few patches that seemed to be a pale beige. It looked so funny that if Val hadn't been so tired and so sorry for the poor animal, she would have burst out laughing.

"Where *is* he going to sleep tonight?" she asked her father. "We can't put him in the infirmary, smelling the way he does. Do you think maybe . . ."

Doc answered her question before she finished speaking. "The garage back home. We can make a bed for him there, and tomorrow I'll try to find some other way of getting the rest of the tar off. Come on, honey — let's get rid of this mess."

In the fading light, they began bundling the tarry rags and fur in the blanket. Mike Strickler came out of Animal Inn as they were shoving the whole thing into a huge plastic garbage bag. The wiry old man trotted over to them and stared at the dog.

"He's sure a sight for sore eyes, ain't he?" he

said. "Donna told me what happened. Good thing you come along, Vallie, 'cause if you hadn't, Del Hoffman prob'ly woulda fallen into that tar pit himself. Del ain't got enough sense to come in outa the rain, if you ask me. Some security guard, lettin' that gate stand open like that! Need any help?"

"You might get another blanket from the storage room, Mike," Doc said. "We're taking the dog home with us. I haven't had time to make up a list of instructions for our patients in the infirmary, but nothing has changed since last night — no new admissions."

"I'll get the blanket, Dad," Val said. "I want to see The Ghost anyway."

She went into the Large Animal Clinic and hurried down the aisle between the stalls until she came to the one where The Gray Ghost lived. It was a big box stall, and on the door was a wooden plaque that Toby had made with The Ghost's name on it. The dapple-gray gelding stuck his head out when he heard her coming and whinnied in welcome.

Ordinarily Val would have put her arms around his neck and given him a big hug, but considering her tarry state and the fact that she smelled strongly of kerosene, she just patted his velvety nose.

"I'm really sorry, Ghost," she said. "I thought we could have a ride today, but there was this dog in trouble and I had to bring him to Dad. I think he's going to be all right, though. We're taking him home with us tonight."

The Ghost's nostrils flared when he smelled the kerosene, and he snorted and tossed his head.

"I'll smell much better tomorrow, honest," Val told him. "And after work, we'll have a nice long ride, I promise. Gotta go now — Mike will take you out into the pasture in a little while." She patted him again, then went to the storage room, grabbed a blanket, and ran for the door, waving at the cow, the sheep, and the goat who were in the other stalls.

"See you later, everybody," she called. " 'Bye!"

When she came out, Doc had pulled the dark blue Animal Inn van into the driveway. Val wrapped the blanket around the dog, then climbed into the back of the van while Mike lifted the animal in beside her.

"Thanks, Mike," she called as the van pulled away. The dog wriggled closer to her and rested its muzzle on her knee. Val patted its spiky head. "Don't worry, boy," she said. "We're going to take good care of you until your owner claims you. I bet you're hungry, aren't you? Well, so am I! Supper's only a few minutes away."

Chapter 3

It was almost dark by the time the van pulled into the driveway next to the Taylors' big stone house on Old Mill Road. Val hopped out and opened the garage doors, then turned on the light inside. Doc's green sedan took up most of the space, but there was just enough room to set up a bed for his latest patient. But what kind of a bed? Val wondered, trying to think what there was in the house that she might use. Erin's doll bed? No, that was much too small. Teddy's toy chest? That wouldn't do, either—the lid might fall down during the night and hit the poor animal on the head. Then Val remembered the old crib that she, Erin, and Teddy had slept in when they were babies. It was still down in the basement somewhere. They could haul it out and set it up out here! It would be perfect — they could put nice soft blankets on the mattress, and the dog wouldn't be able to get out. It would also keep him up off the cool floor. She was just leaving the garage when the back door of the house flew open and a furry black-and-white blur shot down the steps into the yard, barking excitedly. Jocko, the younger of the Taylors' two dogs, was welcoming Doc and Val home.

A moment later Erin dashed out of the house, shouting, "Jocko, you come back here this minute! What's the matter with you . . . oh, Daddy! It's you!" She ran over to give her father a kiss, and stared at the large bundle in his arms. "What's that?" Erin asked. When a blackened, scraggly tail poked out of the blankets and began to wag, she gasped. "It's *alive*!"

"It's a dog," Val told her, "the one that fell into the tar basin this afternoon. We brought him home because we didn't know what else to do with him."

Erin peeled back a corner of the blanket and took a closer look in the light from the garage. "Wow! Is he ever funny-looking!" She wrinkled her nose and backed away. "And does he ever *smell*!"

"I'll have to agree that he's pretty fragrant," Doc said wryly. "We tried to get the tar out of his fur with kerosene, which explains why all three of us need baths as soon as possible. And then we're going to put this fellow to bed out here in the garage. Think you can help your sister find something for him to sleep in?"

Before Erin could answer, Val said, "I know

exactly what to use, Dad — the crib in the basement."

"Good idea," Doc said. "In the meantime, he can lie on this blanket. We'll shut the garage door, though I don't think he's in any condition to make a run for it."

Jocko frisked around Doc's feet as he carried the tar-covered dog into the garage and set him gently down, unwrapping him and rearranging the blanket to make a comfortable pad. The minute Erin saw the whole animal, her eyes widened.

"What happened to his fur?" she cried. "He looks like Jocko did when I tried to clip him like a poodle, only worse!"

"That's because we couldn't get all the tar out of his fur, so we had to chop it off," Val said. "He had really long hair, too. But it'll grow back, won't it, Dad?"

"Indeed it will," Doc said. "Jocko's did, remember."

Hearing his name, the shaggy little mongrel leaped up, trying to lick Doc's face. But then he turned back to the newcomer. It was obvious that he wanted to play and couldn't understand why the other dog just lay there with his muzzle resting on his paws.

"He's all worn out, Jocko," Val explained. "And

you would be, too, if you had the kind of day he's had." She hooked a finger through Jocko's collar and began to lead him away. "Where's Teddy?" she asked Erin as they headed for the house.

"Chasing Ringo," Erin said, brushing back a strand of silvery-blonde hair that had come loose from her ponytail. "He escaped from the Habitrail about an hour ago, and Teddy's afraid Cleveland will find him first and eat him up."

"That Ringo!" Val sighed. "He's the slipperiest hamster I ever knew. But my cat wouldn't eat him — he might play with him for a while, but I'm sure he wouldn't *eat* him. Unless he hadn't had supper, that is . . ."

"He did," Erin said. "I fed him myself, and he ate every single bite. But Teddy's afraid Cleveland might want to have Ringo for dessert!"

"I found him!" Teddy yelled as Val, Erin, and Doc came into the kitchen. Val's eight-year-old brother was clutching his pet in both hands, beaming from ear to ear. The Phillies baseball cap he always wore was perched on top of his golden-brown curls, and a frightened hamster's tiny head poked out from between Teddy's grubby fingers. "You'll never guess where he was! He was on the bookshelf in Dad's study between *Veterinary Medicine for the Rude Practicer* and *Sheepish Diseases*!"

Doc grinned. "I think you mean *Veterinary Medicine for the Rural Practitioner* and *Sheep Diseases*, Teddy, but I'm glad you found him. How about putting him back with John, George, and Paula? I bet they're wondering where he's been."

"I will in a minute. Hi, Vallie. Erin and me ate already, but there's plenty left for you and Dad." Teddy really looked at Val and Doc for the first time since they had come in. "Hey, you guys are all covered with black stuff! You look pretty weird. And you stink something fierce. What happened to that dog Mrs. Racer told us about?"

"He's in the garage," Doc said. "Vallie and Erin are going to dig out your old crib for him to sleep in, and while they're doing that, I'd like you to fill the tub for him so we can give him a good bath. Think you can do that — *after* you put Ringo back in the Habitrail?"

"No problem," Teddy sang out. He trotted off with his hamster, and Val sniffed the air.

"Mmm . . . smells delicious."

"Pasta with zucchini and tomatoes and lots of other good stuff," Erin said. "Even *you* can eat it, Vallie — no meat or anything." Val was the only vegetarian in the family, and Mrs. Racer was always looking for recipes in the local paper that would provide proper nourishment for Val and for everyone else. "C'mon—let's go down to the basement and pull out the crib. And then you and Daddy can wash up after the dog has his bath. What's his name, anyway?"

Val shrugged. "Search me. Nobody's claimed him yet. As far as we're concerned, he's an orphan."

"An orphan! If he were a girl, we could call him Orphan Annie. But since he's a boy, maybe we should call him . . ."

"Orphan Andy?" Val suggested. She was only joking, but Erin laughed and clapped her hands.

"Orphan Andy! That's a terrific name! Little Orphan Andy! That's what we'll call him."

"Until his real owners turn up," Doc put in. "Then we'll have to call him whatever his real name is."

Val and Erin had already started down the stairs to the basement. Doc followed, and so did Jocko. It was only then Val realized that Sunshine, their golden retriever, was nowhere in sight.

"Where's Sunshine?" she asked as she and Erin helped Doc haul the sections of the crib out from behind a pile of boxes.

"Probably sleeping under the dining room table," Erin replied. "He sleeps all the time lately — I guess that's because he's getting old. How old *is*

Sunshine anyway, Daddy? I keep forgetting. I know he's older than me."

"He's one year older than you, honey," Doc said. "He's twelve. Your mother and I adopted him from a litter at the Humane Society Shelter when Vallie was just a baby." He smiled a little sadly, and Val knew he was remembering their beautiful golden-haired mother, who had died three years ago in an automobile accident. She remembered, too, and so did Erin. Before she married Doc, Mrs. Taylor had been a featured dancer with the Pennsylvania Ballet. Erin looked just like her, and she wanted to be a ballerina when she grew up. Val was sure she would be. Erin's ballet teacher, Miss Tamara, said that Erin was the most promising pupil she'd ever had.

"This crib is absolutely *filthy*," Erin said, wiping her dirty hands on her jeans. "We'd better wash it off before we set it up in the garage."

Doc nodded. "Good idea. But let's do it fast. I'm as hungry as a bear, and the sooner we get the crib, the dog, and ourselves cleaned up, the sooner Vallie and I can eat."

It was almost nine o'clock before Val and Doc finally sat down at the butcher-block table in the kitchen. Orphan Andy was as clean as Erin's elderflower shampoo could make him, and Val, Teddy, and Erin had taken turns with the blow dryer to make sure that what was left of his tarry fur wasn't the least bit damp. Val had offered him some canned dog food, but Andy hadn't eaten very much. Like Sunshine, all he wanted to do was sleep. So they put him to bed in a nest of fluffy blankets in the crib and went back to the house.

It had taken more than elderflower shampoo to remove the tar from Val and Doc, but now they were clean at last. Mrs. Racer's pasta disappeared in record time, along with the salad Erin had made, and several helpings of cherry cobbler.

"How come you could scrub all that black stuff off *you*, but Andy's still sticky?" Teddy asked as Doc sipped his coffee and Val enjoyed a cup of herb tea.

"Because the tar is still stuck to Andy's fur," Doc told him. "Fortunately, people aren't furry. If they were, we'd probably look as . . ."

"Weird?" Erin suggested.

"Well, as *peculiar* as Andy does," her father said.

"So why don't you shave him?" Teddy said cheerfully. "Then he wouldn't have any fur, either!"

"But he'd look even weirder," said Val. "And he'd probably catch cold, wouldn't he, Dad?"

"Very possibly." Doc finished his coffee and stood up. "Teddy, it's past your bedtime. Go on up and get into your pajamas — I'll tuck you in."

"Aw, gee, Dad . . ."

Doc gave him a stern look. "*Scoot*, Teddy."

Teddy scooted. A second later, he was back in the kitchen. "Can Ringo sleep with me tonight? I think he's still scared 'cause he thought Cleveland was gonna eat him."

"Ringo has John, George, and Paula to keep him company. He'll be just fine. *Pajamas*, Teddy."

"Oh, okay." Teddy stomped off, and Doc turned to his daughters.

"What's the homework situation, girls?"

"I did all mine," Erin said, "right after ballet class." She began clearing the dishes from the table and stacking them in the dishwasher.

Val groaned. "I haven't even *thought* about mine. I'm supposed to write an essay about what I did on my summer vacation. And I told Jill I'd call her tonight — or she said she was going to call me. I forget, what with all that's been going on. I'd better get moving."

"I have homework, too, believe it or not," Doc said, handing Erin his empty coffee cup. "There are a lot of veterinary magazines that have been piling up over the past few weeks, and if I don't get caught up, I might miss something. Maybe there's an article about removing tar from animal hair — you never know."

Doc went upstairs to tuck Teddy in and then to his study. Val helped Erin clean up the kitchen. As she was scrubbing down the counter, her large orange cat stalked into the room. But instead of rubbing against Val's ankles and yowling to be picked up the way he usually did, Cleveland leaped up onto the table and began to wash himself just as though she weren't even there.

"What's the matter with you?" Val asked, going over to him and trying to rub his ears. Cleveland ordinarily loved having his ears rubbed, but not tonight. He turned his back to her and sat staring out the window, lashing his tail.

"Well, *excuse* me!" Val sighed. "Okay, I get the message. You're mad at me because I didn't find you and cuddle you the minute I got home, right?"

"Cleveland's mad at everybody," Erin said. "Teddy hollered at him for chasing Ringo, and then he sneaked into my room and I was afraid he was going to attack Dandy, so I hollered at him, too."

Val grinned. "Poor Cleveland. Sounds like you had a really bad day — no hamster snacks, and no canary tidbits!" She went into the pantry and took a little box from the shelf. Shaking it so the contents rattled loud enough for Cleveland to hear, she said, "Listen — Kitty Kutlets, your favorite treat. If I give you some, will you be my friend again?"

Erin rolled her eyes. "Honestly, Vallie! You talk to that cat as if he were a person! I'm going to get ready for bed. Are you coming, too?"

"I'll be there in a few minutes," Val said as she opened the box. Cleveland, who had apparently decided to forgive her, was purring like an engine. And after the third Kitty Kutlet, he was his old affectionate self.

"Oh, sure. Now you're my *best* friend," Val laughed, scooping up all twelve furry pounds of cat and cuddling him in her arms. "Come on, Cleveland. Let's go upstairs."

As Val draped her cat over one shoulder and came into the dining room, Sunshine walked slowly over to meet her. His plumy tail was waving and he was smiling his friendly, doggy smile. Val leaned down to pat him.

"Hi, Sunshine. Sorry I don't have time to hang out with you right now," she said, "but I have to say good night to Erin, and then I have homework to do. You're lucky you're a dog — no homework!"

The golden retriever followed her through the living room and into the hall. "Want to come up with me, boy?" Val asked.

Sunshine seemed to be considering it, but then he flopped down on the floor, resting his muzzle on his paws.

"Okay. See you in the morning." Val patted him once more, then bounded up the steps to the second floor. "I wonder what Sunshine will think of Andy," she said to Cleveland. "Oh, I forgot. You don't know about him. Well, I'm going to be calling Jill before I write my essay for English to tell her how I found him and everything, so you can listen."

"Vallie, can you please turn out my light?" Erin called.

"I'm on my way," Val called back. She went into her bedroom and plopped Cleveland down on the bed. "Be back in a minute." Then she paused, looking at the big orange cat. "I can't help wondering what *you'll* think of Andy!"

Chapter 4

Early the next morning, Cleveland let Val know exactly what he thought of their visitor. As usual, Val was the first one up and dressed. Then she grabbed a can of dog food from the pantry and hurried out to the garage with Cleveland at her heels. Waving at the rabbits in their hutch, and the chickens and Archie the duck in their pen, she went inside, eager to find out how Andy was feeling.

Cleveland streaked around her and jumped up on the hood of Doc's car. He took one look at the scruffy animal in the baby crib and crouched down, hissing and spitting.

"Cleveland!" Val said with a frown. "Behave yourself! Is that any way to treat a guest?"

"Raaoow!" said Cleveland. His ears were flattened to his head, and every hair on his body was standing on end, making him look even bigger than he actually was.

Andy stood up on his hind legs with his front

paws on the top rail of the crib and began to bark. Hearing all the noise, the chickens and the duck began to cluck and quack. Val clapped her hands over her ears. "Quiet down, you guys!" she yelled.

Andy's barking turned into excited whines as Val came over and patted his spiky head. Cleveland lashed his tail, mumbling cat curses to himself.

"I'm ashamed of you, Cleveland," Val said sternly. "You act like you've never seen a dog before. You've lived with dogs all your life. Why are you acting this way?"

"*Mrmrmblrm,*" growled Cleveland.

Val decided to ignore him. "How are you doing, Andy?" she said to the dog. "Did you have a good night's sleep?"

In the bright daylight coming through the garage window, Andy looked even stranger than he had last night. Tufts of tarry fur stood up in clumps all over his body. Val thought that his black nose looked like a blob of tar in the middle of his face. She couldn't help it — she started to giggle.

"I'm sorry," she told him. "I know animals hate to be laughed at, but you look so *funny*!" The dog began to lick her hand with his long pink tongue. His scrawny tail was wagging happily. "How about some breakfast?" Val suggested. "I brought you some dog food."

"Yeeeoowrow," said Cleveland, narrowing his golden eyes.

"I'll feed you later," Val said to her cat, pulling the ring that popped the lid of the dog food can. She was about to dump the contents of the can into the bowl Doc had left in the crib last night, when she saw that the food they'd given Andy when they put him to bed was still almost untouched.

"You didn't eat anything at all," she sighed. "What's the matter, fella? Lost your appetite?"

"I wouldn't be surprised." Doc had come into the garage without Val's noticing. Now he patted Cleveland and came over to stand beside her at the crib. " 'Morning, honey." He kissed Val on the cheek. "I don't imagine you'd be very hungry either if you'd fallen into a tar pit and didn't know where your family was." Scratching Andy behind the ears, he added, "I think I'll take him to Animal Inn with me this morning and run some tests. I just want to make sure there's nothing else wrong with this pup."

"Is he only a puppy?" Val asked. "He's so big, I thought he was a full-grown dog."

"From what I saw of his teeth yesterday and from the size of his paws compared to the rest of him, I think he's probably not more than nine months old," her father said. "Andy's going to get a lot bigger before he stops growing."

Val stared at Andy. "Wow! He's going to be *humongous*!"

"Hey, where *is* everybody?" Teddy hollered from the back porch. "I'm starvin' like Marvin! What's for breakfast?"

"Guess we'd better get back to the house before the neighbors start thinking I'm not feeding my children," Doc said, smiling at Val. "When you come out to Animal Inn today after school, I'll give you a full report on Andy's health. But Andy himself might not be there," he added.

Val frowned. "What do you mean?"

"I mean that it's entirely possible that Andy's owner will have found out what's happened to him and where he is. They might come and claim him."

"Oh. Yeah, I guess you're right." Val looked down at the puppy. She knew she should be happy to think that Andy's owners would take him back home, but somehow she wasn't. Andy was a really nice dog. "What if they don't?" she asked.

"Then we'll have to take him to the shelter," Doc said. "The Humane Society will put him up for adoption."

"Breakfast's ready," Erin shouted from the back porch. "I made sausages and scrambled eggs and toast. If you don't come right away, Teddy'll eat everything — unless Jocko beats him to it," she added over the little dog's excited barking.

"Come on, Cleveland." Val picked up her angry cat and headed for the house. "Time for your breakfast, too. That'll make you feel lots better."

"Rraaoow," said Cleveland, giving Andy a dirty look over Val's shoulder.

It was only after Teddy and Erin had hurried off to catch the school bus that Val remembered her bike. Everybody had been so busy taking care of Andy last night that both she and Doc had forgotten all about it.

"I'll drop you off on Codorus Avenue, honey," Doc said, "and then go straight to Animal Inn. I want to check Andy out before office hours begin. Better take him for a walk, and then we'll put him in the van."

Since they had thrown Andy's sticky black collar away, Val used one of Sunshine's old collars. It fit Andy's neck perfectly. Then she snapped one of the dogs' leashes onto it and lowered the side of the crib so Andy could get down. As he trotted out of the garage at her side, Val noticed that he was limping a little.

"What's wrong, boy?" she asked. "Does your leg hurt?"

The pup whimpered softly, but he was in such

a hurry to get outside that Val didn't take time to look closely at his legs. Besides, Doc would be giving him a complete examination this morning. If there was anything the matter with Andy, he would be sure to find it.

Doc lifted the puppy into the back of the van. As Val climbed into the passenger seat she told him about Andy's limp.

"I'll examine him from nose to tail," Doc promised. "And I'll give you a full report when you come to the clinic after school."

A few minutes later, the van pulled up in front of the highway department enclosure. The tall gates were wide open, and big trucks were lumbering out with their loads of tar and gravel. Doc waited while Val went in to make sure her bike was still there. It was, so he waved and drove away. Val could see Andy standing up, peering out of the back window.

As she mounted her bike and started off for school, she wished she were going to Animal Inn instead. It seemed like a very long time until three o'clock. Then she'd be able to find out if there was anything really wrong with the big, funny-looking pup.

To Val's surprise, the school day didn't drag at all. It was good being back with all her friends, many of whom she hadn't seen all summer long. The only person Val *wasn't* glad to see was Lila Bascombe. Lila didn't like Val one bit, and Val didn't like her, either.

"I don't believe you and Toby Curran were the ones who cracked the petnapping ring," Lila said after school as Val was going to get her bike from the rack. Val had been one of the students Mr. Steele had called on to read their essays aloud during English class. "I bet you just made it all up so you'd get a good grade."

Val smiled sweetly. "If you'd been here last month instead of visiting your grandmother in Harrisburg, you'd have read all about it in the *Essex Gazette*."

Mr. Steele had called on Lila, too. She had tried to make her vacation sound exciting, but what it all boiled down to was that Lila had spent the entire month of August with her grandmother, going to every store in Harrisburg, shopping for new clothes. That didn't sound like much fun to Val.

"I had more *important* things to do," Lila said, tossing her head.

"Right." Val got on her bike and began pedaling to Animal Inn. Lila was a royal pain, but today she didn't bother Val at all. Val had more *important* things on her mind — like Andy. What if his owner had found out where he was and had taken him home? Or what if he was still there, but Doc had discovered that he was sick?

Twenty minutes later, Val leaned her bike against the white rail fence surrounding the parking lot in front of the clinic. She was about to go in the side entrance when Donna Hartman stuck her head out of the grooming salon window.

"Yoo-hoo! Vallie! Come in here — I have something to show you," Donna said. Her eyes were sparkling, and she sounded excited. Ordinarily Val would have been glad to visit what Toby always called the "beauty parlor," but today she was so anxious to find out about Andy that she didn't want to stop for anything. Before she could make an excuse, Donna was holding the door open.

"It'll only take a minute," she said, grinning. "I know you're in a hurry."

Val didn't want to be rude, so she followed Donna inside.

"Look!" Donna said proudly.

Val looked. What she saw was a large, skinny dog standing in the middle of the room. His pale beige fur had been clipped short everywhere but on his head. His furry face was black around the eyes and white around his muzzle, but beige everywhere else. His drooping ears were black, and his nose was black, too — like a blob of tar. When he saw Val, his tail began to wag.

Val just stared at him. "It's not — it couldn't be — that's not *Andy*, is it?" she squawked.

Giggling like a little girl, Donna said, "It's him, all right. Cleaned up pretty good, isn't he?"

Val kneeled down beside the pup and put an arm around him. "But how — what did you — how did you. . . ?" She was so astonished that she couldn't finish a sentence.

"Mayonnaise," Donna said, wiping her hands on her flowered smock.

Val blinked. *"Mayonnaise?* You're kidding!"

"Nope. That's what did the trick." Donna lowered herself into a chair. "See, Jim and I went to the supermarket last night after work, and the minute I saw the mayonnaise sitting there on the shelf, I remembered something I'd read in that 'Household Hints' column in the *Gazette* a while back. It said mayonnaise was good for removing tar, so we bought two great big jars of it. And since things were pretty slow today, I worked on Andy here all afternoon. Then I clipped him to kind of even out his fur, and *then* I gave him a nice shampoo, a moisturizing rinse, and a skin conditioning treatment." She beamed at Val and Andy. "If I do say so myself, he looks real nice."

"Oh, Donna, he looks *wonderful*!" Val cried. She gave Andy a hug and the puppy licked her face. "Kind of like a big, wooly lamb. Has Dad seen him yet?"

"He sure has. Doc took him to the treatment room a little while ago to put that bandage on his leg."

Val had been so stunned and delighted by the sight of Andy that the bandage hadn't registered until now. It was an elastic bandage like the one she sometimes used when she threw her knee out playing softball, and it was wrapped around the puppy's left hind leg.

"Did Dad say what's wrong with his leg?" she asked Donna.

"Something about some kind of fracture showing up on the X rays," Donna said. "But it's not real bad. He'll tell you all about it when you see him, I guess."

Val leaped to her feet. "I'll go find him right away!" She ran over to Donna and kissed her cheek. "Thanks for making Andy look so terrific."

Donna's face turned almost as pink as her bright-colored lipstick. "I like to see animals looking nice," she said. "I think they feel better when they're clean, too, just like people. You can leave Andy here for now, Vallie. He's no trouble at all."

"Okay. I'll get him in a little while," Val promised. "And thanks again," she added as she hurried out the door — and almost bumped into Toby. "Have you seen him?" she asked eagerly. "Doesn't he look great?"

Toby stared at her. "Who are you talking about?"

"Andy! The dog that fell into the tar pit, remember?"

"Oh, him. Yeah, I saw him. He looks pretty good," Toby said.

"It just proves what I keep trying to tell you," Val said smugly. "Donna's grooming operation isn't all that silly after all."

Toby grinned at her. "Okay, okay, you win. Are you gonna get to work or what? I'm on my way to cover for Pat while she takes her break, and Doc could use some help with that pet raccoon I just took into the first treatment room."

"Yes, *sir*!" Val gave him a snappy salute. Then she snatched a white lab coat from a peg in the hall and put it on over her T-shirt and jeans. Maybe while she was giving Doc a hand with the raccoon, he could tell her about Andy's leg.

As it turned out, however, the raccoon was so terrified by his first trip to the vet that calming him down took all of Doc's and Val's attention. Then there was another animal to attend to, and another, and another. It wasn't until the last patient had left, and Animal Inn was officially closed for the day, that Val was able to ask her father about the pup.

"His main problem is malnutrition," Doc told her. "His bones are very brittle, and one of them fractured fairly recently, from the look of it. It probably happened when he was struggling to get out of the tar basin. But because he's so young, it will knit all by itself, provided we keep the leg bandaged and keep Andy quiet. All he needs is a healthy diet and plenty of rest, and he'll be just fine." He leaned down to pat the puppy, who was sitting at Val's feet on the floor of Doc's little office.

"Then I guess we can't take him to the shelter right away, can we?" Val said hopefully. "I mean, it wouldn't be fair to bring them an animal that needed medical care and a special diet and stuff, would it?"

"Vallie, we are *not* adopting this puppy," Doc said. "Three dogs is one dog too many. And for all we know, his owner will turn up any day now. I placed an ad in the paper telling anyone who had lost a large, long-haired puppy in the vicinity of Codorus Avenue to contact Animal Inn."

Val looked down at Andy and grinned. "I bet they'd never recognize him now! But I wasn't talking about adopting him, Dad. I just meant that until he's well enough — maybe we could take care of him at home. And *then* we'll take him to the shelter.

Doc rubbed his beard. "I guess we could. We'll have to consult Mrs. Racer, though. We don't want to make extra work for her."

"She won't have to do anything for Andy at all," Val assured him. "He'll be my own special project. You can tell me what to do for him, and I'll do it. I'll make a bed for him in my room so the other dogs and Cleveland won't bother him. If Mrs. Racer says yes, can we do it?"

Smiling, Doc said, "Okay, Vallie. Consider Andy your own personal private patient."

"Terrific!" Val kissed him on the cheek. "Did you hear that, Andy?" she said to the pup. "Welcome to Animal Inn's Annex!"

Chapter 5

On Saturday morning, Val introduced Andy to Mrs. Racer. They took to each other at once.

"The poor thing!" Mrs. Racer crooned, fondling the puppy's silly-looking ears. "I won't mind having another animal around the house, Vallie. It gets awful quiet during the week when you and Teddy and Erin are in school. This pup and me will get along just fine."

Andy waved his skinny tail and licked the old lady's hand.

"See that! We're friends already," Mrs. Racer said. "Don't you worry about a thing, Doc. You and Vallie had better get going, or all your patients will be waiting on the doorstep for Animal Inn to open." She smoothed the skirt of her simple black-and-white print dress. "M'son Henry's coming by in a little while to take Erin and me to the market, and we'll drop Teddy off at Billy's house on the way. We'll take Erin to ballet class afterward, too. And then this little fella and me will have the rest of the day to get to know each other."

"Thanks, Mrs. Racer," Doc said. "But if by the end of the day you've changed your mind, you be sure and tell us."

The old lady smiled. "I will, but I won't, if you know what I mean."

"There's one other thing," Val said, glancing at Cleveland. The cat was sitting on the kitchen counter, glaring down at Andy through slitted eyes. "Cleveland's not exactly crazy about Andy. You'd better keep an eye on him just in case he decides to turn into an attack cat. And Jocko's *too* crazy about him — he wants to play with him all the time, but Andy needs to be real quiet and get plenty of rest. Maybe you could keep an eye on Jocko, too."

"No problem," said Mrs. Racer cheerfully. "Anything I ought to know about Sunshine?"

Hearing his name, the golden retriever under the kitchen table wagged his tail.

"I don't think so," Val said. "Sunshine doesn't seem to care one way or the other. But he doesn't know Andy very well yet so . . ."

"I'll keep an eye on all four of 'em, Vallie," Mrs. Racer promised. "And when you and Doc come home tonight, I wouldn't be surprised if they were all one big, happy family."

But they weren't, not that evening nor the next day nor the next week. Cleveland made it very clear that as far as he was concerned, Doc was right — three dogs was one dog too many. Bouncy little Jocko still couldn't seem to get it through his head that Andy was in no condition to be a playmate and spent most of his time chasing Cleveland instead. Sunshine continued to mope and kept out of the puppy's way as much as possible.

"You're acting very silly," Val told him sternly after Andy had been living with the Taylors for ten days. "The only reason Andy gets special treatment is because he's not well. And since nobody's claimed him, he really *is* an orphan. He's not going to be here forever, you know. As soon as he's healthy again and his leg is all better, we're taking him to the Humane Society Shelter. Until then, can't you stop being jealous and be nice to him?"

Sunshine just looked at her out of his big brown eyes and whimpered softly.

Val sighed. There had to be something she could do to make Sunshine and Cleveland feel better about Andy. And suddenly she knew exactly what it was.

On Sunday she put her plan into operation. She

managed to round up Teddy and Erin before Teddy ran off to play with his friends and Erin disappeared into the basement to practice her ballet.

"Listen, guys," she said when her brother and sister had plopped themselves down in the living room. "Having Andy here presents a real problem as far as Sunshine and Cleveland are concerned. . . ."

"Better believe it!" Teddy said as he wrestled on the floor with Jocko. "Sunshine's no fun anymore. All he does is sleep and hide from Andy."

"And Cleveland's being just *awful,*" Erin added. "Every time he sees Andy, he hisses and blows himself up like a balloon. Not only that, but last night he didn't use his litter box!"

"I know." Val sighed. "I had to clean up the mess he made in the upstairs hall right outside my room. From what I've read in Dad's magazines, that's the way cats show that they're unhappy about something."

"Even though you sprayed lots of air freshener, it smelled *awful,*" Erin said.

"It stank something fierce," Teddy put in. "Is he gonna keep doing that for as long as Andy's here?"

"That's what I want to talk to both of you about," Val said. "Andy's my special private patient, and I want to take good care of him so he can go to the shelter real soon. But until that happens, all of us have to help make Cleveland and Sunshine understand that we don't love them any less than we did before Andy came."

"*I'm* beginning to love Cleveland a *lot* less," Erin said, wrinkling her nose.

"Well, you shouldn't," Val said, frowning. "We have to be super nice to all our pets. Because I'm not here very much, I can't do a lot for our other animals, so that means that you and Teddy have to show them how much we care about them."

"Like how?" Teddy asked.

"Like taking Sunshine for extra walks, and giving Cleveland kitty treats and snuggling him a lot." Val looked down at Jocko. "Jocko's no problem — all we have to do with him is make sure he doesn't try to play with Andy too much."

"Okay, we'll do it," Erin said. "Now can I practice my Snowflake dance?"

"And can I *please* go meet Erin and Billy?" Teddy asked. "I'll take Sunshine for a long, long walk when I get back, honest."

Val shrugged. "Okay. But remember what I said. It's really important."

"We'll remember," Teddy and Erin said together. Then Teddy shot out of the house, pulling on his jacket as he ran. Erin headed for the basement.

"*Raaooow!*" said Cleveland. He was sitting on

the fireplace mantel staring down at Andy, who was snoozing at Val's feet.

Val went over and picked up the cat, and Cleveland promptly dug his claws into her shoulder and hissed.

"Now Cleveland, cut that out!" she said. "You're my only cat and I love you very much, but you definitely have an attitude problem." Holding Cleveland up so that she and the cat were nose to nose, Val went on, "It's time you realized that Andy isn't the enemy — he's just a poor, sick puppy, and we all have to be nice to him while he's here. *All* of us, including you. Understand?"

"Mmmmmmrrrrmmm," Cleveland muttered.

"I've been reading up on animal psychology," she told the cat, "and all the articles say that it's important to pay lots of attention to family pets when there's a new animal in the house. So today I'm going to spend a lot of time playing with you and Sunshine, and Jill's going to help me. She's coming over in a few minutes." Val tickled Cleveland under the chin, and was rewarded by a faint purr. Smiling, Val said, "That's more like it."

She picked up the brand-new catnip mouse she'd bought the day before and tossed it on the sofa. "Look, Cleveland, a present just for you!"

Cleveland leaped onto the sofa and sniffed eagerly at the mouse. With one swipe of his paw, he snatched it and began rubbing his face against it, purring more loudly.

Suddenly the front door flew open and Jill burst into the living room. "Sorry I'm late for the pet therapy session," she chirped. "Hey, I see you started without me — that first patient is already on the couch! I thought you were going to be a vet, Val, not a pet shrink!"

Val grinned at her friend. "Cleveland's pretty happy right now. Why don't you tackle Sunshine? I think he's in the dining room, under the table. Here — " She tossed a rubber ball at Jill. "This is Sunshine's favorite toy. He loves to retrieve it when you throw it for him."

"That doesn't sound too hard. I think I can handle it," Jill said, tossing the ball in the air. She headed for the dining room, which was separated from the living room only by a wide arch. Bending down, she waved the ball under Sunshine's nose. "C'mon, boy — want to play catch?"

The golden retriever's tail wagged, but he didn't come out from under the table.

"Throw it to him," Val suggested.

Jill threw the ball. It bounced against Sunshine's nose, but Sunshine didn't react. He didn't even watch it roll into a corner under the china cabinet.

"What do I do now?" Jill asked.

"Fetch it," Val called. "Throw it to him again."

Jill did. Sunshine closed his eyes and rested his head on his paws.

"Val, I don't think this dog is interested in playing ball." Jill sighed as she retrieved the ball from under one of the chairs in the living room. "Got any other ideas about how I can make Sunshine happy?"

Val giggled. "Maybe we ought to change places. Cleveland's having a catnip fit. Why don't you hang out with him and I'll play with Sunshine?"

"Good idea." Jill tossed the ball to Val. "I know more about cats than I do about dogs anyway."

Val went into the dining room and got down on hands and knees next to Sunshine.

"Want to play?" she asked, offering him the ball. She threw the ball into the living room. "Go get it, boy!" she urged. "Fetch!"

Sunshine stayed where he was, but Jocko squirmed out from under the sofa and dashed after the ball. He picked it up in his mouth and headed for the stairway in the hall.

"Jocko, you come back here!" Val called, running after him. "That's Sunshine's toy . . ."

"Val, look out!" Jill yelled as an orange blur streaked across Val's path. It was Cleveland, in hot pursuit of Jocko. Jill's warning came too late — Val tripped over the cat and landed on the floor, knocking over a small end table. The crash woke Andy, who struggled to his feet and started barking.

Cleveland leaped on top of the television cabinet, hissing and spitting at the pup, and Jocko came galloping back downstairs to see what all the fuss was about. He'd dropped the ball somewhere along the way, and now he was barking as he raced back and forth between the angry cat and the excited puppy.

"What's going on down there?" Doc called from the top of the stairs.

At the same time, Erin ran into the living room. "Vallie, are you all right?" she asked, staring down at her sister on the floor. "What happened?"

Val got up and set the table back on its legs, then snatched Cleveland from the television cabinet and smoothed his ruffled fur. "I'm okay," she told Erin. "Everything's fine, Dad," she shouted. "Sorry if we interrupted your baseball game." Doc had been watching the Phillies game on the television in his second-floor study. "Who's winning?"

"The Phillies — I think," Doc called back. "All that commotion made me lose track of the score. How about a little peace and quiet for a change?"

Jill had snagged Jocko's collar and was holding the little dog on her lap, calming him down. Andy's frantic yelps were quieting down, too.

"That's better," Erin said with a sigh. A muffled whimper from the dining room made her look around. Sunshine was still lying under the table, looking sorrowful.

"Oh, poor Sunshine," Erin cried. She went over to him and bent down, reaching out to pat his golden head. "You don't like all that noise, do you? Well I don't, either. I could hardly hear the music I was dancing to."

By now, Jill was dissolved in giggles. "Oh, Val," she gasped, "you looked so funny! It was just like one of those old Marx brothers movies . . ."

Val gave her a dirty look, and Jill tried very hard to control herself. "You didn't really hurt yourself, did you?" she asked.

Rubbing her rear end, Val said, "Not really." Then she grinned. "Who would have ever thought pet therapy would turn out to be so dangerous?"

"Pet therapy?" Erin echoed. "Is that what you were doing?" She looked down at Sunshine. "If you were trying to make Sunshine feel better, I don't think it worked."

"I don't think it did, either," Val said. She rubbed Cleveland's ears, but the cat struggled to escape, and she let him leap out of her arms. "But we have to keep trying," she told Erin. "It's not going to be easy, but we have to show Sunshine and Cleveland that having Andy in the house won't make any difference at all."

Val couldn't help wondering, though, if she'd taken on an impossible task.

Chapter 6

One week later, the animals weren't getting along any better in spite of Val, Doc, Teddy, Erin, and Mrs. Racer's efforts. Even though Andy was getting better every day under Val's constant care, neither Cleveland nor Sunshine were willing to accept the big puppy with the funny-looking ears as a member of the family. Cleveland continued to hiss and curse every time he saw the pup, and Sunshine looked sadder and sadder. He ate even less and didn't seem to enjoy his walks. His golden coat was becoming dull and dry.

"Dad, do you think maybe Sunshine is sick?" Val asked one night after the old dog had refused to eat anything at all. She and her father were sitting in his study, and Sunshine was dozing on the floor at Doc's feet.

"I've been thinking the same thing myself," Doc said. "A certain amount of jealousy is natural in a case like this, but Sunshine seems to be carrying it to extremes. It's not time for his regular checkup, but perhaps we ought to take him to Animal Inn and give him some tests."

The following day, Doc did just that. Val came in after school, eager to learn the results. Since Doc was busy with a patient, she looked for Toby and found him giving the animals in the infirmary their afternoon medications.

"What's happening with Sunshine?" she asked as Toby popped a pill into the mouth of a wriggling schnauzer.

"Don't know," Toby said. He made sure the schnauzer had swallowed the pill, then moved on to the next cage. "Doc sent a bunch of blood tests to the lab and they haven't come back yet."

"What kind of tests?" Val asked. "Here — let me take care of Screwball." She checked the chart Toby was holding and took a pill from the little paper cup with Screwball's name on it. The fluffy gray cat greeted her with delighted mews and tried to swipe the medicine out of Val's hand with one speedy paw. Val grabbed the cat, tucked her under her arm, and gave her the pill almost before Screwball knew what was happening.

Toby shrugged. "You got me. All I know is that Sunshine's blood samples went to the lab in Harrisburg along with a bunch of others and we won't know anything until tomorrow."

Val put Screwball back into her cage, latched the door, and went on to the next patient, a yellow-and-white mongrel named Skippy. "So you don't know what Dad was testing Sunshine for?" she asked.

"Nope." Toby shoved a dropper filled with antibiotic into Skippy's mouth, squeezed it, and patted the dog. "I don't know any more than you do."

For some reason, Val didn't believe him, and she told him so. "That's not true. You *do* know something, Toby Curran, and I want to know what it is. Sunshine's *my* dog, after all."

"Maybe you better ask Doc," Toby mumbled. "I *don't* know what's going on with Sunshine, because Doc didn't tell me, and that's the truth. But he did a lot of other tests, and I've been working at Animal Inn long enough to know that . . ."

"That what?"

Toby strode away, pushing the medication cart and saying in a very low voice, "That he thinks Sunshine's very sick."

Val gasped. "But he can't be! Sunshine's hardly ever been sick a day in his life. He's just out of condition because he hasn't been eating right — he's *jealous*, not sick!"

"Like I said, you better talk to Doc." Toby opened another cage and held out a pill to the dog inside. The dog gobbled it up as though it were candy.

"I sure will!" Val started out of the infirmary, then paused. "You have to be wrong, Toby," she said. "You haven't been working here nearly as long as I have, so maybe you don't know that Dad always runs lots of tests on older animals just to be on the safe side. It doesn't mean Sunshine's in bad shape. Dad's just being careful."

But as she went in search of her father, Val felt a cold knot of fear tighten in her chest.

Val found Doc in the Large Animal Clinic. Ordinarily she would have stopped to talk to The Gray Ghost and to give him a treat. But today she only patted his nose as he stuck his head out over the door of his stall and hurried down to where Doc was checking on a sad-looking sheep.

"Hi, Dad. How's Dolly doing?" she asked.

Doc glanced up. "Hi, honey. She's much better today. Darned if I know how she managed to get enough lead in her system to bring her down, but the treatment seems to be working. You can call Mr. Slater and tell him to pick her up tomorrow afternoon." As he came out of Dolly's stall, he added,

"Speaking of calling, aren't you supposed to be covering the reception desk so Pat can take a break?"

"Oh, yeah, I guess I am." Val had completely forgotten about it in her worry about Sunshine. "I'll relieve her in a minute. But first, tell me about Sunshine. You don't think there's anything really wrong with him, do you?" Doc didn't reply. Val kept pace with her father as he headed for the barn door. "Do you think maybe he's anemic? I bet that's it — you can give him some iron and vitamin shots and then he'll be fine, right?"

"We'll talk about it later, honey." Doc held the side door of the clinic open for her. "You take over for Pat now," he told Val. "And you can send the next patient in. I'm running a little behind today."

He went into the first treatment room, and Val slowly entered the reception area. She was really worried now. It wasn't like Doc to avoid answering her questions, particularly questions about animal care. If he didn't want to talk about Sunshine, something was definitely wrong. She decided to pin him down as soon as Pat got back from her break, no matter how many patients were waiting to see him.

But the waiting room was filled with animals and their owners, and the minute Pat saw Val, she told her that she was coming down with a terrible cold and asked if Val would mind covering the reception desk for the rest of the afternoon.

"You know how I am when I get one of my colds," Pat said, snuffling into a tissue. "But if I can just go home and soak in a nice hot tub, I think I'll be much better by tomorrow."

Val sighed. "That's okay, Pat. You go ahead — I'll take over."

The plump little woman picked up her purse from under the desk and hurried off, sneezing and blowing her nose.

It was almost half past five by the time the last patient had been cared for. Toby had left a little early, so there was nobody left at Animal Inn but Val, Doc, and Mike Strickler.

"What's the matter, Vallie?" Mike asked, leaning on his broom and peering closely at Val as she locked the waiting room door. "You're lookin' a little peaked. Not gettin' sick, are you?"

Val shook her head. "No, I'm okay. I've got something on my mind, that's all."

"Worryin' about that there dog of yours, I bet." Mike started sweeping again. "I seen him layin' in Doc's office. What's wrong with him?"

"I don't know," Val said. "I thought he was just sulking because he's jealous of Andy, but Toby thinks he's sick."

"Andy — is that the pup you're takin' care of at home?" Mike asked. When Val nodded, he went on, "Could be. Old animals is just like old folks — they don't like change much. 'Course, if Sunshine *is* sick, your dad'll know just what to do for him. Doc Taylor's the best vet in these here parts, and don't you forget it!"

Val smiled. "Dad's the best vet, period. But I can't help worrying about Sunshine. He's twelve years old, you know."

"Twelve? Is that all?" Mike snorted. "Why, that's less than ninety in people years. Look at me — I was a hundred and six my last birthday, and I'm still going strong!"

Val couldn't help laughing. "Oh, Mike, last month you said you were a hundred and ten!"

Mike grinned at her, his eyes twinkling. "Well, what if I did? Us old folks tend to forget things sometimes."

Still smiling, Val said good night and went into Doc's office. Her father was sitting behind his cluttered desk, finishing up some paperwork, and Sunshine was lying on the floor. The golden retriever wagged his tail and slowly got to his feet when he saw Val. As she bent down to pat him, she noticed that his eyes looked dull, and his nose felt warm.

"Are you ever going to tell me what you think

is wrong with him?" Val pleaded, looking her father straight in the eye. "Is he just run down, or is he really, really sick?"

Doc rubbed his short, graying beard. "Vallie, you know I never make a diagnosis until I have all the facts, and at the moment, I don't. When Sunshine's test results come back, I'll be able to put the pieces of the puzzle together."

"That means there *is* a puzzle," Val said quickly. "Won't you at least tell me what you suspect?"

Doc came around the desk and put his hands on her shoulders. "It doesn't look good, honey," he said gently. "Sunshine's lymph nodes are enlarged and so is his spleen. From those and other indications, I'm very much afraid that he may have . . ."

"Cancer?" Val whispered. "Oh, no, Dad!"

"I said he *may* have," Doc repeated. "I haven't ruled out other possibilities, so I don't want you getting all upset. I probably shouldn't have told you." He looked into Val's tear-filled eyes and sighed. "Now I wish that I hadn't."

Val took a deep breath. When she could speak, she said, "I *made* you tell me. If I'm going to be a vet like you, I have to know things like this so I can help."

Doc gave her a hug. "Yes, I suppose you will.

It's not the easiest career in the world, you know. A vet has to be both tender and tough — sometimes *very* tough."

He released her, and Val found Sunshine's leash under some papers on Doc's desk. She fastened it to the dog's collar. "Guess we'd better be getting home," she said around the lump in her throat. "Mrs. Racer will be wondering where we are."

Doc gave Mike his instructions for the night. Then he, Val, and Sunshine got into the car and started for home. They drove in silence for a while, both lost in the same sad thoughts. Finally Doc said, "I don't want to worry Teddy and Erin about Sunshine's condition. That means I'm going to need your help, Vallie. Think you can put on a cheerful face?"

Val forced a smile. "I can if you can," she said. She knew how badly Doc must be feeling because he loved Sunshine justas much as she did. She glanced into the backseat where Sunshine was sitting, looking out the window. In the dim light she could almost convince herself that there was nothing the matter with him at all.

After all, Val thought, it was possible that he *didn't* have cancer — not even Doc knew for sure. Maybe Sunshine had something else, something that wasn't so awful. Val remembered Charlie, the cat that belonged to Teddy's friend Sparky. Charlie had been so sick that everyone thought he was going to die, but Doc had saved his life.

And Charlie wasn't the only animal Doc had cured when it looked like there was no hope left. Not that there was no hope for Sunshine, Val told herself firmly. No way! Even if it turned out that he had cancer, that didn't mean he couldn't get better. Doc could give him chemotherapy and radiation treatments. It was wonderful what modern medicine could do, and Doc knew all the latest techniques. Doc was the best vet there was. No matter what was wrong with Sunshine, Val was absolutely positive that her father could make him well.

Chapter 7

Teddy met them at the door when Val, Doc, and Sunshine arrived home that night.

"Want to hear a Halloween joke, Vallie?" Teddy asked as he gave his father a hug and a kiss. "It's a real good one — Billy told it to me. Why couldn't the ghost go out on Halloween night?"

"I give up," Val said.

"Me, too," Doc added. "I haven't heard a good joke in a long time."

"Because he didn't have a *haunting* license!" Teddy grinned at them. "Get it? Like a *hunting* license, only because he's a ghost . . ."

"I get it," Doc said with a smile. "But isn't it a little early for Halloween jokes? It's still only September." He leaned down to pat Jocko, who had romped into the hallway to welcome them home. Jocko was especially glad to see Sunshine. The two dogs had hardly ever been separated in all of Jocko's short life.

"It's not really too early," Erin called from the

living room. "One of the girls in my class already handed out invitations for her Halloween party today. It's going to be in Sharon's basement. And she asked Olivia and me to help her with the decorations. We're going to turn the basement into a spooky cave with bats and skeletons and everything."

"Yeah, and Sparky's mom says she can have a party, too," Teddy said. "It'll be *lots* scarier than dumb old Sharon's!" He ruffled Sunshine's golden fur. "I'm gonna take you and Jocko trick-or-treating with me this year," he told the dog. "I don't know what I'm gonna be yet, but whatever it is, you guys will be my mascots."

Sunshine wagged his tail and licked Teddy's hand.

"I know exactly what I'm going to be for Halloween," Erin said, as Val and Doc came into the living room. "I've been thinking about it for months and months. I'm going to be Sleeping Beauty in a beautiful tutu and Mommy's tiara that she wore when she danced as the Sugarplum Fairy with the Pennsylvania Ballet. Mrs. Racer's going to help me make my costume. What're you going to be, Vallie?"

Before Val could reply, Teddy said, "If you're gonna be Sleeping Beauty, you'll have to keep your eyes closed all the time. Maybe *you* oughta take Sunshine with you as a seeing-eye dog!"

"I'm going to be Sleeping Beauty *after* she wakes up," Erin told him, tossing her head. She patted the old golden retriever. "Did you give Sunshine an examination, Daddy? Is he okay?"

"Where's Andy?" Val asked quickly. "Is he still up in my room?"

"I guess so. I haven't seen him since I got home," Erin said. "And I think Cleveland's in the kitchen with Mrs. Racer."

"Cleveland's having his supper," Mrs. Racer said, coming into the living room. She had taken off the apron she always wore over her plain cotton dress, and was tucking a strand of silver hair under her little white lawn cap. "That cat won't eat a bite if Andy's anywhere around, so I fed him early. Evening, Doc, Vallie. How's Sunshine?"

"Pretty well, considering his age," Doc said. He and Val avoided each other's eyes. "Everything all right on the home front, Mrs. Racer?"

Mrs. Racer smiled. "Just fine, Doc. Supper's ready any time you are. Vallie, you want to help Erin set the table? And Teddy, mind you finish that report you're supposed to be doin' for homework tonight." A horn honked outside, and she said, "That's m'son Henry. I'll be runnin' along now. See you all tomorrow."

" 'Night, Mrs. Racer," Teddy said as he opened

the door for her and grabbed Jocko's collar so the little dog didn't run out after her.

"Maybe you'd better feed Sunshine before you let Andy out of your room," Erin said to Val. "He's like Cleveland — he doesn't like to eat with Andy in the room. Teddy can help me set the table."

"Do I hafta?" Teddy asked his father. "That's a girl's job!"

"In this family, there're no such thing as girls' jobs and boys' jobs," Doc told him, giving a playful tug to the visor of Teddy's Phillies baseball cap. "You ought to know that by now."

"Yeah, I *know* it, but I don't hafta *like* it," Teddy grumbled on his way to the kitchen.

While he set the table and Erin began serving dinner, Val patted Cleveland, then opened a can of dog food for Sunshine. He sniffed at it, but he didn't seem very interested.

"Sunshine's getting awfully skinny," Erin said. "Are you sure nothing's the matter with him?"

"Old dogs don't eat very much," Val replied. "They don't need a lot of food because they're not very active."

"Andy eats like a *horse*," Teddy said. "And he's not very active, either. But I guess that's because he's just a puppy and he's growing. How big do you think

Andy's gonna get, Vallie? Will he be as big as Sunshine?"

Val shrugged. "Maybe bigger. We don't know what kind of dog he is. If he's part sheepdog, he could grow up to be huge."

She went upstairs to let Andy out of her room. After she had helped him come down the steps, she sat down at the kitchen table with Doc, Teddy, and Erin. Although the macaroni and cheese that Mrs. Racer had made for her was delicious, Val didn't have much of an appetite. She pretended to eat as Teddy and Erin talked about what was happening at Jackson Elementary School and in Erin's ballet class.

Val kept glancing down at Sunshine, who was lying under the table with his head resting on her foot. Andy sat next to her chair, his bright brown eyes taking in everyone. It seemed like only yesterday that Sunshine was young and full of energy. He was the very first pet Val could remember. For a while, he was much bigger than she was! But he was always so gentle. . . .

"Vallie, wake up! You haven't heard a word I said," Erin complained.

Val blinked. "Sorry. Daydreaming, I guess. What did I miss?"

"Nothing much," Teddy said through a mouthful of food. "Erin was just talking about some dumb dance she's gonna do for the old folks at the retirement home."

"Teddy, please don't talk with your mouth full," Doc said mildly but firmly.

"And it's not 'some dumb dance,' " Erin said. "Some of Miss Tamara's star pupils are going to put on a holiday show at Homewood right before Thanksgiving, and Olivia and I are going to be in it! Miss Tamara's going to announce it in class tomorrow."

Val smiled. "That's great. But if she's not announcing it till tomorrow, how do you know?"

"Because Olivia's mother ran into Miss Tamara at the grocery store this afternoon and Miss Tamara told her and she told Olivia and Olivia told me. But we're going to act very surprised when she tells everybody else."

"Are you gonna do a turkey dance?" Teddy teased. "Gobble, gobble, gobble! I always *knew* you were a turkey, Erin!"

"*Daddy . . . !*" Erin wailed.

"That's enough, Teddy." Doc stood up and began collecting everyone's plates. When he came to Val's, he said, "You didn't eat much, honey."

Val sighed. "I tried. I'm just not very hungry, that's all."

"I'll get dessert," Erin said. "Do you want some, Vallie?"

Val shook her head. "I don't think so. My stomach doesn't feel too good. May I be excused, Dad? I have some homework to do so I might as well start on it. But I'll help Erin clean up after you're through, okay?"

When her father nodded, Val bent down and patted Sunshine. Then she picked up Cleveland, who was, as usual, sitting on the counter giving Andy dirty looks, and left the kitchen. On her way out, she heard Erin saying, "What's the matter with Vallie, Daddy? Do you think she's getting sick?"

"No, honey. She's just tired. And she has a lot on her mind, what with school and taking care of Andy . . ."

And Sunshine, Val thought. Most of all, Sunshine.

The following day wasn't one of Val's regular days at Animal Inn, but she had to know if Sunshine's test results had come back, so she biked out there right after school. It was a beautiful, sunny September afternoon.

"Hi, Vallie," Pat Dempwolf said when she came into the waiting room. "Going to take that horse of yours for a ride?"

"Maybe later," Val replied. "I need to talk to my dad. Do you know where he is?"

Pat smiled. "He's between patients right now. I think he's in his office, checking out some lab reports that just came in."

"Thanks, Pat." Val headed for Doc's little office. She found him sitting behind his cluttered desk, looking at some papers.

"Hi, Dad," she said. "I guess you know why I'm here."

Doc looked up. His expression was very solemn. "Yes, I do. Sit down, Vallie."

Val sat, clenching her hands tight in her lap.

"It's not good news, is it?" she asked in a small voice.

"No, it's not." Doc put the papers down. "I'm going to give it to you straight, honey. Sunshine has lymphosarcoma — that's a form of cancer that is fairly common in dogs. Nobody knows what causes it. And in an old dog, it's very serious."

Val bowed her head, clasping her hands even more tightly.

"You mean it could kill him?" she asked.

"It could." Doc leaned back in his chair, wearily rubbing his eyes.

Val jumped up from her seat. "But chemotherapy and radiation can save him, isn't that right? He could live for *years* yet, couldn't he?"

Doc nodded. "Maybe not for years, but perhaps for a few more months. *Maybe*. They wouldn't be good months, Vallie. The side effects . . ."

"But he'd be *alive*! You're going to do it, aren't you, Dad?"

When Doc didn't answer immediately, Val leaned over his desk. "You're not just going to let him die, are you?"

Doc looked up at her. "No, honey, I'm not. But I don't think you understand that Sunshine is probably in a lot of pain right now. Unlike people, animals don't complain much when something hurts. So unless there's something wrong with them that we can actually see, like a broken leg or a wound, we don't always realize how badly they're feeling." He paused, then went on. "Sometimes there comes a time in an animal's life when it's kinder, more humane, to end its suffering."

Val's eyes widened. "You mean you want to put Sunshine to *sleep*? You can't! You just *can't*! Vets are supposed to *save* animals' lives, not end them! Remember when Mr. Merrill wanted you to put The Ghost down? You wouldn't do it! You *can't* kill Sunshine — you just can't!"

"That was a different matter. The Ghost was not in bad shape. He couldn't see well enough to compete in the show ring, but otherwise there was nothing wrong with him that couldn't be fixed. But Sunshine . . ."

"No!" Tears began to pour down Val's cheeks. "I won't let you do it! Sunshine deserves every chance he gets! You *can't* kill him! I won't let you!"

Doc reached out to touch her hand. "Honey, believe me, I don't want to do it. I love Sunshine as much as you do. But as I told you the other day, veterinarians have to be tough. They can't let personal emotions stand in the way of doing what is best for an animal. And sometimes the best thing is . . ."

"To kill it?" Val wrenched her hand away. "I can't believe it. I *won't* believe it. Not Sunshine! He's not just a dog, he's a member of the family."

Doc sighed. "I know, Vallie." He took the red bandanna he always carried out of the hip pocket of his jeans and held it out to her. Silently, Val took it and wiped her eyes. "This is one of the aspects of veterinary medicine that I've always shielded you from," he went on. "I'm very proud and happy that you want to be a vet — you know that." Val nodded. "But you're very young, and I didn't want to burden you with the hardest part of my profession. Every time it becomes necessary for me to put an animal down, it makes me very, very sad. I don't talk about it, though, and I always make sure neither you nor Toby are around when it has to be done."

"But I always knew," Val said around the lump in her throat. "You'd be very quiet when you came home, and then whatever animal it was never showed up at Animal Inn again. I knew, but I just didn't want to think about it. I still don't!" She took a deep breath. "Dad, please don't give up on Sunshine yet. *Please* try everything you can do to keep him alive! Every time I read the articles in your medical magazines, they've discovered some new drug or treatment or something for all kinds of awful diseases. It would be so terrible if you put Sunshine to sleep and then somebody came up with a cure for the kind of cancer he's got. *Please*, Dad!"

Doc got up, came around his desk, and put his arms around her. "All right, honey. I'll do what I can for him. But I have to warn you that sometimes the treatment is almost worse than the disease."

Resting her head on his chest, Val said, "It *can't* be worse than dying. Remember what you always say? All life is valuable. That means Sunshine's life is valuable, too."

"There has never been the slightest doubt in my mind about that," Doc said.

Just then Pat's voice came over the intercom. "Doc, Mr. McAdams is here for Spike's three-thirty appointment."

Doc released Val and pushed the intercom button. "Be right there, Pat. Ask Toby to take Spike into the first treatment room." Turning back to Val, he said, "Why don't you go for a ride on The Ghost? It's a beautiful day, and I think your horse has been feeling kind of neglected lately."

"I guess maybe I will." Val gave the bandanna back to her father. Then they left the office. Doc headed for the first treatment room and Val went out the side door heading toward the barn.

But in spite of the warm September sun, she felt chilled inside. Sunshine was very sick. What if Doc couldn't make him well? What if he had to put him to sleep, anyway?

Val shivered. "Maybe I'm not cut out to be a vet after all," she whispered to herself.

Chapter 8

Doc began Sunshine's treatment the very next day. He and Val agreed that it would be better not to tell Teddy and Erin how sick their old friend really was. It would only worry and upset them, and there was nothing they could do to help him get well. Val decided not to tell Jill, either, so the only people who knew were herself, Doc, and Toby. Because he spent so much time at Animal Inn, Toby was familiar with all of Doc's patients and their problems. When Doc began bringing Sunshine to the clinic every few weeks for chemotherapy and radiation, he knew exactly what was wrong.

"I'm really sorry, Val — about Sunshine, I mean," Toby said one afternoon in early October. "Do you think he's going to get better?"

"Of course he is," Val snapped. "Sunshine's going to be just fine. Dad's the best vet there is, you know that. Now are you going to take Mrs. Murphy's cat out to her, or do you want me to do it?"

Toby picked up Mittens Murphy. The gray-and-white cat was still groggy from the anesthesia after Doc had pulled four of his teeth. "I'll do it. But about Sunshine . . ."

"Toby, I don't want to talk about it, okay? I told you he's going to be all right!"

Val hurried off to get Doc's next patient from the waiting room. She hadn't meant to snap at Toby, but somehow it was easier to deal with Sunshine's illness when she didn't speak to anybody about it, not even Doc. Hearing Toby say he was sorry only reminded her of how slim the dog's chances were. Val didn't need reminding.

As the weeks went by, Sunshine seemed to be getting thinner and weaker. Erin and Teddy noticed it, too.

"Yes, Sunshine's having some health problems," Doc told them. "As dogs get older, they need a lot of special attention. That's why I'm bringing him to Animal Inn regularly for checkups and tests. Sunshine's not feeling very well right now, but I don't want you to worry about him."

"Dad's taking real good care of him," Val added.

That made her younger brother and sister feel better. Besides, they were so wrapped up in their various activities that they didn't have time to pay much attention to anything else — except Andy, who got stronger and bouncier with every passing day.

Doc was pleased with the pup's progress, and so was Val. Watching Andy's health improve under her care made her feel less uncertain about wanting to be a vet. Soon they'd be able to take the bandage off his leg, and then Doc would take him to the Humane Society Shelter where some kind person would adopt him. But Val didn't want to think about that, either.

Then all of a sudden in mid-October, when the leaves on the trees had turned from green to red, orange, and gold, Sunshine started looking better. His appetite began to improve, his eyes lost that dull, listless glaze, and even his dry, patchy coat seemed glossier and thicker. When Doc weighed him on his next visit to Animal Inn, Sunshine had gained almost a whole pound.

"I knew it!" Val cried happily, writing down the dog's weight on his chart. "He's going to get well! You saved his life, Dad!"

Her father smiled. "Sunshine's a fighter, that's for sure. And I think he knows how much we love him. Animals respond to loving care just the way people do. We'll continue the treatment, and keep our fingers crossed."

Val laughed. "That doesn't sound like a very scientific statement to me."

"You're right," Doc admitted. "But then, medicine isn't an exact science, Vallie. Doctors like to pretend it is, but there are a lot of factors that knock all of our calculations into a cocked hat. Attitude is one of them. And Sunshine has a very positive attitude."

"So do I!" Val said, stroking the dog's golden head.

"I know, honey. Believe me, I know."

Now that Sunshine was feeling better, Val was able to stop worrying about him and start thinking about Halloween.

"Do you think we're too old to go trick-or-treating?" she asked Jill. They were having lunch in the Hamilton Junior High cafeteria with their friends Sarah, Alison, Lisa, and Robin.

"I don't know," Jill said, biting into her taco. "Just because we're teenagers doesn't mean we can't have fun the way we used to."

"I don't know about you guys," Sarah said, "but *I'm* going. I *love* trick-or-treating — except for all those boys who go around spraying shaving cream on anything that moves!"

"Has anybody been invited to Lila Bascombe's Halloween party?" Robin asked.

Everybody groaned.

"Not me," Alison said. "And if she *did* ask me, I wouldn't go. Kimberly told me she's going to have kissing games and yucky stuff like that."

Lisa gagged. "Gimme a break! Can you imagine kissing Butch Fisher?"

"Or Robert Ford?" Val said, making a face. "Robert's braces would probably cut your lips to pieces!"

"So let's go trick-or-treating," Sarah suggested. "I don't care about all that candy and stuff, but it's neat running around town after dark and checking out all the costumes. And you could all come to my house afterward — my folks wouldn't mind. Speaking of costumes, what's everybody going to be?"

Alison said she was going to be a hamburger. Lisa was going to be a rock star with pink hair, Robin planned to dress up like Dorothy in *The Wizard of Oz*, and Jill was going to be Cleopatra. "What's your costume, Val?" Jill asked.

Val shrugged. "I haven't really thought about it yet." She munched her veggie burger while she considered a costume. Suddenly she had an idea. "Maybe I'll be a scarecrow. I could wear jeans and one of Dad's old shirts, and I could stuff myself with straw from the barn at Animal Inn! Are you really going to have a party, Sarah?" she asked her friend.

"Sure. Why not? We'll have lots more fun than the kids at Lila's party. And if I invite any boys, I promise there *won't* be any kissing games!"

"Invite Toby Curran," Jill said. "He's one of Val's best friends, even though he doesn't go to our school. Toby's really nice."

"Do you think he'd come, Val?" Sarah asked. "And if he does, do you think he might bring some ice cream from Curran's Ice Cream Parlor?"

"I don't know," Val said. "Toby hangs out with the guys from his school most of the time. He might think it was silly to go to a Halloween party. But I'll ask him if you want me to."

"And I'll ask Jimmy Dunkle and Lewis Morgan," Robin put in. "Hey, this is really going to be fun! Eat your heart out, Lila Bascombe!"

"I think I'm gonna be Rambo," Teddy said the following night. "Or maybe a robot. Or maybe I'll be a spaceman from Mars — or maybe . . ."

Erin sighed. "Honestly, Teddy! If you don't make up your mind soon, you'll end up wearing one of our old sheets with holes cut out for the eyes the way you did last year. Mrs. Racer's almost finished with my Sleeping Beauty costume. It's going to be absolutely beautiful! I hope it's not so cold that I'll have to wear a coat over it when we go trick-or-treating."

"If you do, you'll be able to take it off when you get to Sharon's house," Doc said, lowering the newspaper he'd been reading. "And if Sharon's giving prizes for the best costume, I'm sure you'll win."

"Thanks, Daddy." Erin beamed at him. "I think I will, too. What's Sparky going to be for Halloween?" she asked her little brother.

Teddy made a face. "A *princess*. Can you beat that? She's gonna have a dumb crown and everything. She's gonna look pretty silly with those pigtails sticking out from under a princess crown!"

Sitting on the floor between Sunshine and Andy, Val grinned. "Maybe she won't be wearing pigtails with her princess costume. You shouldn't make fun of her, Teddy. She *is* a girl, you know."

"Yeah, I know. But I keep trying to forget." Teddy got off the sofa and went over to the televison. "Dad, can I turn on the TV? We had our dinner and I finished all my homework and it's time for my favorite show."

Doc nodded. "Okay. But after it's over, I want you to go right up to bed, understand?"

Teddy flopped down on his stomach and pressed

the buttons on the remote control. Jocko lay down beside him as *World Warriors* came onto the screen.

Val stood up. "I guess I'll call Toby," she said. "Sarah Jones is having a Halloween party and I'm supposed to ask Toby to come, but I forgot when I was at Animal Inn today." Andy and Sunshine followed her into the kitchen. Val hadn't really forgotten to tell Toby about the party — it was just that ever since she'd refused to talk to him about Sunshine, Toby had avoided her as much as possible. Val realized that his feelings were hurt. Maybe asking him to the party would make him understand that they were still friends, and that would be easier to do over the phone.

"Oh, hi, Val," Toby said when he answered. "What's up?" He didn't sound very happy to hear her voice.

"Nothing much. I was just wondering if you'd like to come to a Halloween party a week from next Friday," Val told him.

"How come?" Toby asked suspiciously.

Val sighed. "What do you mean, 'how come'? It's no big deal. All you have to say is yes or no."

"I mean how come you're inviting me? You've hardly even *spoken* to me for weeks."

"*You're* the one who hasn't been speaking to

me," Val said. "Hey, this is silly. We're acting like a couple of little kids. I wouldn't have asked you to come if I didn't *want* you to come."

Looking down, she saw that Sunshine had ambled over to his dish and was eating some of his food left over from supper. That made her smile.

"And by the way, in case you haven't noticed, Sunshine's a lot better. The last time Dad weighed him . . ."

"He had gained twelve ounces. I saw his chart," Toby put in. "That's great." Now he sounded more like himself. "About this party — thanks for asking me, but I can't come. There's a square dance at my school, and afterward my brothers and I are having some of our friends over. Just guys," he added quickly, "or else I'd have invited you."

"Okay," Val said. "What's your costume going to be?"

"Costume?" Toby sounded shocked. "I'm not wearing any costume. That's kid stuff! But my little brother Jake's gonna be a pirate, or maybe an astronaut. He can't make up his mind."

"Neither can Teddy." Val decided not to tell him that not only was she planning on wearing a costume, but she was going trick-or-treating as well. "See you tomorrow at Animal Inn. If it's nice, want to ride The Ghost for a while after office hours?"

"That'd be neat. Night, Val. See you tomorrow."

As Val hung up the phone, she felt good. Sunshine was better, she and Toby were friends again, and she was looking forward to Sarah's party. Everything was working out just fine!

Chapter 9

Two days before Halloween, Val was helping Teddy and Erin carve scary faces in their pumpkins when the telephone rang. Val answered it, and heard Pat Dempwolf's excited voice.

"Vallie, guess what?" Pat said. "Jim Hartman just called from the hospital — Donna had her baby! It's a girl, seven pounds five ounces. And you know what they're naming it? Valentine! Isn't it wonderful?"

Val felt her cheeks turning pink. "That *is* wonderful, Pat," she cried. "Thanks for telling me. Are they both okay?"

"Couldn't be better, from what Jim said," Pat told her. "He's coming to Animal Inn tomorrow to pass out cigars!"

Val giggled. "Gee, Pat, I didn't know you smoked cigars."

"Oh, Vallie, you're such a tease . . . oops, the other line's flashing. I have to go now. I just thought you'd want to know about the baby."

"Thanks, Pat," Val said again. " 'Bye."

The minute she hung up, Erin said, "What's wonderful? What happened?"

"Pat smoked *cigars*?" Teddy asked, his eyes nearly as big as the ones he was cutting into his pumpkin.

When Val explained about the baby, Teddy was disappointed — it wasn't his idea of exciting news. But Erin was thrilled.

"I think it's terrific that they named her after you," she said happily. "I'm going to make Donna a pretty card just as soon as I finish my jack-o'-lantern. Maybe Donna and Jim will let me baby-sit when Valentine's a little older. I wouldn't charge much, and it would be fun taking care of a cute little baby!"

Teddy started cutting out his pumpkin's nose. "Sounds pretty boring to me. Babies don't *do* anything — they just lie there and yell and stuff."

Val grinned at him. "Nobody's asking *you* to baby-sit, Teddy. But it would be nice if you made a card for Donna and Jim, too."

"Gimme a break!" Teddy groaned. Then he brightened. "I could make a Halloween card with a real little jack-o'-lantern on it. A baby one, with no teeth!"

Val and Erin both laughed, and even Sunshine,

who had ambled into the kitchen to see what all the fuss was about, wagged his plumy tail and smiled.

After school, Val and Mrs. Racer helped Erin and Teddy get into their costumes. Teddy had decided to be an android from his favorite TV show, *World Warriors*, and had bought his costume at the dime store the day before. Val and Mrs. Racer handed out homemade popcorn balls and cookies to the little ghosts, goblins, and witches who came to the door, while Erin and Teddy went trick-or-treating with their friends.

Then, after Olivia and her mother had picked up Erin to take her to Sharon's party, and Val had walked Teddy to Sparky's house, it was time for Val to put on her costume. She stuffed her rattiest jeans and one of Doc's oldest shirts with straw, painted on a scarecrow face, put on a battered felt hat she'd found in the attic, and joined Jill and their friends for some trick-or-treating of their own.

They ended up at Sarah Jones's house along with several other kids from Hamilton Junior High. Mr. and Mrs. Jones provided plenty of food for their hungry guests. Everyone had a great time listening to rock music, bobbing for apples, and pretending to be scared when Sarah turned out all the lights and passed around slimy things that she said were slugs, worms, and fresh blood, but turned out to be avocado slices, cold spaghetti, and tomato juice.

Val and Jill agreed that it was a great party. "But I'm glad Toby didn't come," Val confessed. "If he'd seen me in my scarecrow outfit, I'd never have heard the end of it!"

A week after Sarah's party, Val noticed a change in Sunshine.

"Dad, he's losing weight again, isn't he?" she asked her father after Sunshine's regular examination. "He's almost stopped eating and his fur's starting to fall out, too."

Doc rubbed his beard. "I was afraid this might happen, honey, but I didn't want to worry you so I didn't mention it. Remember when I said we ought to keep our fingers crossed?"

Val nodded, stroking Sunshine's head.

"It sometimes happens when an animal has cancer that his disease goes into what is called spontaneous remission. We don't know why — it might be a result of the treatment he's been getting; but on the other hand, it's been known to happen in an animal that's had no treatment at all. For a while, the animal seems to be on the road to recovery. . . ."

When he didn't continue, Val said, "And then what?" though she was afraid she knew the answer.

"And then — well, its health deteriorates very rapidly." Doc reached down and patted Sunshine, too. The dog whimpered, as if even the touch of loving hands were painful to him.

"You mean that in spite of everything you can do, Sunshine's going to get worse and worse," Val murmured.

"I'm afraid so," Doc said. "I can probably keep him alive a while longer, but it won't be much of a life. He's in pain now, and it can only get worse. The treatments I'm giving him will be increasingly unpleasant for him as he becomes weaker."

Val swallowed hard. "I'd hate that. But we can't just let him die."

"No, we can't. I think it's time to consider the alternative." Doc put a hand on Val's shoulder. "You know what I'm talking about, don't you?"

Val nodded. "Putting him to sleep." She fought back the tears that stung her eyes. "But it's so *awful*!"

"I know. If I thought there was any way to give him more time — more *good* time — I'd do it. But consider this, Vallie. Sunshine has had twelve happy, wonderful years. If we really love him, and we all do, is it kind to make him suffer for a few more weeks or months? Would we be keeping him alive for his sake, or for our own because we can't imagine *our* lives without him?"

Memories of Sunshine filled Val's head — the big, bouncy golden puppy she'd played with when she was very small; the friendly dog whose cheerful disposition had never failed, even when Teddy was little and pulled his tail or Erin dressed him up in a tutu and tried to teach him to dance.

Looking down at Sunshine as he was now, she knew her father was right.

"I guess we better tell Erin and Teddy," she said softly.

That night after supper Doc called a family conference. When Teddy, Erin, and Val were seated in the living room of the big stone house, he stood in front of the fireplace and looked solemnly at each of his children.

"There's something I want to discuss with you," Doc began.

"Is it gonna take very long? Because I don't want to miss *World Warriors* and it's on in about ten minutes," Teddy said, fidgeting in the big armchair he was sharing with Jocko.

"Mmmrraow?" Cleveland added from his perch on the mantel.

"I don't know how long it will take, Teddy," Doc told him. "It depends on how important you think it is."

Erin glanced from her father to Val. "It's serious, isn't it, Daddy?"

Doc nodded. "Pretty serious, I'd say. I want to talk to you all about Sunshine."

"He's sick again, isn't he?" Teddy said, looking over at the dog lying at Val's feet. "He gets sick a lot lately."

"Are you going to put him in the infirmary at Animal Inn?" Erin asked. "Is that what you want to talk to us about?"

"No." Doc went over to his favorite chair and sat down. Andy trotted over next to him and sat down, too. "Sunshine is a lot sicker than Vallie and I have let you know. He's gotten so sick that he can't get well again."

There was a long silence. Finally Teddy said, "D'you mean he's gonna *die*?"

"Oh, no!" Erin gasped. "You can fix whatever's wrong with him, can't you, Daddy?"

"I wish I could," Doc said sadly, "but I've done everything I can do." In very simple terms, he explained about the treatments he'd been giving Sunshine.

"For a while he seemed to be getting better, but he wasn't really," Val added. "And that's why Dad thinks the best thing to do is . . ." She couldn't bring herself to say the words.

Doc came to her rescue. "What Vallie's trying to say is that rather than letting Sunshine suffer more and more, as he's bound to do, we can show him how much we love him by helping him go peacefully to sleep."

Erin and Teddy stared at their father as the meaning of what he had said sank in. Then tears filled Erin's eyes and trickled down her cheeks. Val could tell that Teddy was trying very hard not to cry, but it was a losing battle. He put his arms around Jocko and buried his face in the little dog's fur, squeezing him so tightly that Jocko let out a surprised grunt.

"You mean . . . you're going to . . ." Erin's voice trailed off, choked by sobs.

"I'm sorry, kids," Doc said wearily. "But if we love him, we have to let him go."

"Will it — hurt him?" Teddy mumbled, still clutching Jocko.

Doc shook his head. "No, Teddy. It won't hurt at all, I promise. What *will* hurt him is forcing him to keep on living when all he knows is pain."

"Dad's right," Val said, blinking back her own tears. "I didn't think so at first, but now I do. It'll be awfully hard for all of us — hardest of all for Dad, because he's the one who'll have to do it and he loves Sunshine as much as the rest of us do. But it'll be easy for Sunshine." She bent down and patted her old friend. She could feel his ribs under the thinning fur.

Doc stood up and stretched out his arms. After a moment, Teddy and Erin ran over to him, hugging him tightly, and so did Val. They stood there holding onto each other. Everyone was crying, even Doc, and Val knew that this was the worst thing that had happened to them as a family since her mother had died. But as long as they had each other, they'd get through it somehow. They had before, and they would again. It hurt, though.

Two days later, on Saturday morning, they buried Sunshine's ashes under the apple tree in the backyard. Mrs. Racer was with them, holding Teddy's and Erin's hands. She had picked a bouquet of late chrysanthemums from the garden, and as Val laid the bright yellow and dark red flowers on the little mound of earth, Mrs. Racer said, "Ashes to ashes, dust to dust . . ."

" . . . show me a friend a friend can trust," Erin said softly. "Somebody wrote that in my autograph book last year. Sunshine was a friend, all right."

Teddy nodded, wiping his nose on the sleeve of his jacket. "He sure was. He was Jocko's *best* friend.

Jocko's gonna be awful lonely without him — and so am I."

"We all will be, Teddy," Doc said, resting a hand on Teddy's shoulder. "But never forget that we did what was best for Sunshine."

Chapter 10

As they stood under the bare limbs of the apple tree, shivering in the cold November breeze, Val heard the faint ringing of the telephone inside the house. She didn't want to answer it, but when it kept on ringing, she sighed.

"I'll get it," she said, trudging to the back porch and up the steps. Jocko and Andy greeted her as she came inside, whining and wagging their tails. They couldn't understand why they were cooped up indoors when everybody else was outside.

Val picked up the phone. "Hello?"

"Hello — is that Val Taylor?" a man's cheerful voice asked. "This is George Frick from the Humane Society Shelter. Is your dad there?"

"Uh . . . he's out in the yard," Val said. "Can I take a message? Is this an emergency? Is one of the animals sick or something?"

"No emergency," Mr. Frick said. "I just wanted to tell Doc that we have room for that pup he told us about some time ago, the one you pulled out of the tar pit. And there's somebody who's interested in him, too. A nice middle-aged couple who want a big young dog; all we've got now are little dogs. Please tell your dad to bring that pup over in the next couple of days and we can almost guarantee he'll have a home."

"Okay, I'll tell him. Thanks, Mr. Frick."

Val hung up the receiver and looked down at Andy. Doc had taken the bandage off his leg, and now he was growling happily, hanging onto one end of Sunshine's old rubber pull-toy, while Jocko held the other end in his jaws. If it wasn't for Andy, Val realized, Jocko would be a very lonely dog, just as Teddy had said. And if Andy found a new home . . .

The back door opened and Doc, Mrs. Racer, Erin, and Teddy came into the kitchen. They all looked very solemn.

"Who was that, Vallie?" Doc asked, taking off his red-and-black plaid lumberjack jacket. Teddy and Erin sat down at the butcher-block table while Mrs. Racer began making hot cocoa.

"Mr. Frick from the shelter," Val told him. "It wasn't an emergency or anything. He just called to say that the shelter could take Andy now, and there's a couple who know about him and might want to adopt him."

"I see." Doc was watching Andy and Jocko just as Val had done. "What did you tell him?"

"I didn't tell him anything. I just said I'd give you the message."

Andy dropped his end of the pull-toy and trotted over to her, jumping up and planting his big, furry paws on her chest. Val pushed him gently down.

"Seems to me like Andy's already got a home," Mrs. Racer said as she stirred the cocoa on the stove. "Erin, you want to get some marshmallows from the pantry?"

Erin got up and headed for the pantry, glancing at her father as she passed him. But she didn't say anything.

Teddy looked up at Doc from under the visor of his Phillies baseball cap. "Jocko likes Andy a lot, Dad. I mean, it's not like he could take Sunshine's place or anything, but — well, Jocko's used to having Andy around, and maybe he wouldn't be so sad if . . ."

". . . if we adopted Andy," Doc finished the sentence for him. "I'm not so sure that's a good idea."

Val removed Cleveland from the kitchen counter so Mrs. Racer could set out the mugs for the cocoa. "I'm kind of used to having Andy around, too. And Cleveland's not nearly as jealous of him as he was when Andy first came — now Andy, cut that out!" she shouted as the puppy chased the cat into the dining room.

"I don't know," Erin said, dropping a marshmallow into each of the mugs. "I don't know if I'm ready to have another dog. We've known Sunshine all our lives, and we've only known Andy for a couple of months."

"I'm inclined to agree with Erin," Doc said. "We're all still pretty sad about Sunshine. I think it's too soon to make a decision about adopting Andy. Meanwhile, if someone is really interested in him, it wouldn't be fair to deny him the chance of a good home while we make up our minds. I'll return Mr. Frick's call when we get to Animal Inn." He checked his watch. "Vallie, we'd better drink that cocoa and be on our way. I told Toby we'd be there by eleven at the latest, and it's almost that now. Erin, we'll drop you off at ballet class on our way."

Erin sighed. "All right. But I don't feel much like dancing today."

When Doc spoke to Mr. Frick, they agreed that Doc would take Andy to the shelter on Monday when Animal Inn was closed. Mr. Frick would arrange for Mr. and Mrs. Baumgartner, the couple he'd mentioned to Val, to come and see the pup either that day or the next. Ordinarily, Val would have wanted to visit the shelter with her father, but this time she was glad he was going while she was in school. And when Mr. Frick phoned on Tuesday night to say that the Baumgartners were delighted with Andy and had taken him home with them that afternoon, Val tried very hard to be happy for him. But the house on Old Mill Road seemed very quiet and empty without Sunshine and Andy. Erin practiced her solo for the holiday show at the retirement home, but her heart wasn't in it. And even though Thanksgiving was just around the corner, Teddy didn't come home with a single turkey joke to make them laugh.

"Who wants to go with me to Stambaugh's Turkey Farm tomorrow to pick up our bird?" Doc asked. It was the Tuesday before Thanksgiving and the Taylors were having supper. "Mrs. Racer tells me Ezra Stambaugh promised to save one of his best ones for us."

"Not me," Val said, shaking her head. "You know how I feel about going out there. It's bad enough seeing the turkeys at Mr. Stambaugh's stand in the farmer's market, but it's even worse seeing them at the farm when all the others are still walking around."

"Yes, I know, Vallie," her father said. "What

about you, Teddy? Erin? I'll be closing Animal Inn early and I could pick you up here around five-thirty."

"Okay," Erin said. "I told Mrs. Racer I'd help her bake pumpkin and mince pies after school, but I'm sure we'll be finished by then."

"Could Sparky come, too?" Teddy asked. "Maybe it'd cheer her up."

Doc raised his eyebrows. "Why does Sparky need cheering up?"

"Because her grandparents were supposed to come for Thanksgiving, but now they can't 'cause they've both got the flu. So Sparky and her mom aren't even gonna have a turkey — they'll probably go to some dumb restaurant," Teddy said. "On second thought, maybe coming with us isn't such a hot idea. It'll just remind Sparky that she's gonna have a sad Thanksgiving."

"We're going to have a pretty sad Thanksgiving, too," Erin sighed. "This will be our first Thanksgiving without Sunshine."

Val had been thinking the same thing, but she hadn't wanted to say anything. Suddenly she had an idea. "Dad, why don't we ask Sparky and Mrs. Sparks to have Thanksgiving dinner with us?" she suggested. "Maybe we can all cheer each other up — or try to, anyway."

"Hey, yeah, Dad!" Teddy's face lit up for the first time in weeks. "Can we? That'd be neat!"

Doc smiled. "You're absolutely right, Teddy. It *would* be neat. Excellent idea, Vallie. I'll call Mrs. Sparks right now."

As he picked up the phone, Erin said, "You did remember to invite Mike, didn't you, Daddy? It would be so depressing if he had to eat at Rose's Diner the way he usually does."

"We asked him last week," Val assured her. "With Gramps and Nana all the way down in Florida, Mike's the closest thing to a grandfather we've got."

"Hello — Catherine?" Doc said into the receiver. "This is Theodore Taylor. I hope I didn't interrupt your supper. . . . That's good. Er — I know this is rather short notice, but my family and I were wondering if you and Sparky would like to join us for Thanksgiving dinner. . . . Yes, Teddy told me that your parents won't be coming after all. . . . No, it wouldn't be any trouble at all. . . . You would? Well, that's just fine! Around one o'clock on Thursday, then. Oh, and Teddy wants to know if Sparky can come with us tomorrow afternoon when we go to Stambaugh's farm to get our turkey . . . about five-thirty. I'll pick the kids up here at the house. . . . You're more than welcome. See you Thursday." He hung up the phone.

"They're coming! Hooray!" Teddy shouted. Then he looked a little embarrassed. "It won't be as good as having Sunshine back, but it's better'n nothing," he mumbled.

Doc gave him a hug. "You don't have to apologize for feeling happy, son. When he was in good health, Sunshine was a very happy dog. We all have to remember that. Then we won't feel so sad."

"I wish we could explain that to Jocko," Val said, looking down at the little black-and-white mongrel. "He misses Sunshine as much as the rest of us do — and Andy, too."

"I wonder how Andy's doing with his new family," Erin said as she and Val cleared the table. "I hope the Baumgartners are good to him."

"From what I understand, everything's working out just fine," Doc said. "I spoke to one of the volunteers at the shelter the other day. She had just been to their house on a follow-up visit to see how Andy was getting along, and she said he seemed to be settling in nicely." He began slicing the applesauce spice cake Mrs. Racer had baked for dessert. "There was one small problem, though . . ."

"What kind of problem?" Val asked, frowning.

"Well, according to Mr. Baumgartner, Andy tries to escape every time anyone opens the door.

They have to watch him like a hawk whenever they go in or out."

Now Erin frowned. "Maybe that means he doesn't like it there."

"Hey, Jocko does the same thing, and he *loves* it here," Teddy pointed out. Just then the phone rang, and he yelled, "I'll get it! . . . Oh, hi, Sparky. What's up? Your mom hasn't changed her mind or anything, has she? . . . Good . . . okay, I'll ask him." Covering the mouthpiece of the receiver, he said, "Dad, Sparky says her mom wants to know if she can bring her extra-special cranberry-orange relish on Thanksgiving. And Sparky wants to know if *she* can bring Charlie."

"Yes, and no," Doc said firmly.

"Cleveland doesn't much care for other cats," Val reminded her little brother. "But you can tell Sparky that we'll give her some turkey to take home to Charlie so he doesn't feel left out."

Teddy relayed the message and then sat back down at the table with the rest of the family. "Sparky says okay," he said, digging into his piece of cake. "She didn't think you'd let Charlie come, but she thought she'd ask anyway."

"Let's see . . ." Instead of eating her dessert, Erin began making notes on the pad Mrs. Racer used for her grocery list. "There'll be seven people for Thanksgiving dinner. Since you're not going to the turkey farm with us, Vallie, you can help Mrs. Racer wash the good china, and when we get back, Teddy and I will help polish the silver. And Daddy, you'll have to put the extra piece in the dining room table so it'll be big enough for all of us . . . Mrs. Racer's going to make the turkey stuffing tomorrow, the kind with nuts and celery and apples in it. Maybe tomorrow morning, before you go to school, Teddy, you could pick some apples from our tree. There aren't many left, but there ought to be enough for the stuffing. . . ." She looked up from her scribbling and smiled. "You know, it's been a long time since we had guests for dinner. This is going to be fun." Then her face fell. "Or it could be, if only . . ."

"It *will* be fun," Val said quickly. "It's like Dad said — it's okay to be happy, Erin. It doesn't mean we've forgotten Sunshine."

"I'll *never* forget Sunshine," Teddy said. "Jocko won't either, I bet."

Under the table, the little dog wagged his tail, but it wasn't a happy wag. Val wished there was something she could do to cheer him up — lately the only thing he enjoyed doing was chasing Cleveland, and that wasn't making Cleveland very happy.

Maybe after a little while, Doc would let them get another dog from the shelter, Val thought, one that needed a loving home. If only the Baumgartners hadn't adopted Andy. . . . But they had, and that was that.

Chapter 11

At a few minutes to one o'clock on Thanksgiving Day, the Taylor house was filled with the delicious aroma of roasting turkey. Even Val had to admit that it smelled good, though she would never eat a bite of it. But she certainly wouldn't starve! Besides the little casserole of stuffing that had been baked outside the bird, especially for her, there were turnips, mashed potatoes, creamed onions, and corn, not to mention celery, carrot sticks, Mrs. Racer's famous watermelon pickles, and the mince and pumpkin pies Erin had helped bake.

Before she went home on Wednesday evening, Mrs. Racer had written out a list of instructions on how to prepare the meal. All the Taylors had gotten up very early Thursday morning to do the cooking, and now they were ready to greet their guests.

Mike Strickler was the first to arrive. "Gee, Mike, you look great," Teddy said as he opened the door, being careful to block Jocko's usual attempt to dash outside.

"You seen this here suit before," Mike replied with a grin. "It's the only one I got! You don't look so bad yourself, young fella. Your dad hide your baseball cap?"

"Not exactly, but he said it didn't look good with my turtleneck and slacks," Teddy told him. "I feel kinda bald without it, though."

They came into the living room, where Val, Erin, and Doc wished Mike a happy Thanksgiving.

"A real handsome family you got here, Doc," Mike said. "Vallie, I keep forgettin' how pretty you look in a dress!"

Val blushed, and Erin said, "That's what I keep telling her, but she only puts one on for special occasions."

The doorbell rang again, and Teddy flung the door open while Val held Jocko's collar. "Hi, Mrs. Sparks! Hi, Sparky — gosh, *you're* wearing a dress, too!"

"Mom made me," Sparky said. "And don't you dare make fun of me, Teddy Taylor, or I'll . . ."

"That's enough, Philomena," her mother put in. "Try *not* to act like a tomboy just for today, okay?"

After Erin hung up their coats, Doc introduced Mrs. Sparks and Sparky to Mike. When Val took the container of cranberry-orange relish Mrs. Sparks had brought into the kitchen, Mrs. Sparks followed her.

"Won't you let me do something to help?" she asked.

"Oh, no. You're our guest," Val said, tying one of Mrs. Racer's aprons over her dress. "Guests are supposed to enjoy themselves. Erin and I can manage just fine."

Mrs. Sparks smiled at her. "I'll let you in on a little secret, Val. I *love* to cook, but because I work full-time, I almost never have the chance. My housekeeper, Mrs. Wilson, does most of the cooking for Sparky and me. If you really want me to enjoy myself, find me another apron!"

"Well, okay, if you're sure." Val took an apron from the drawer where Mrs. Racer kept them and handed it to her. As Mrs. Sparks put it on, Val realized that it was one of the ones her mother used to wear. It was kind of funny to see it on somebody else.

"Vallie, you have to come out here!" Erin called from the dining room. "Jocko's acting really strange!"

"What do you mean, strange?" Val said, coming out of the kitchen. But before Erin had a chance to answer, she saw what her sister meant. Jocko was galloping back and forth from the living room to the dining room, jumping up at every window and peering outside. His tail was wagging wildly, and as he leaped up to look out the dining room window, he began to bark.

"Sorry, everybody," Doc said, striding over to the dog. "Jocko's not usually so badly behaved. *Down*, boy!" he commanded, but Jocko paid no attention.

"Maybe he sees a squirrel," Val said as she came over to the window. "You know how he is with squirrels." She looked out the window too — and gasped. "It's *not* a squirrel!" she cried. "It's Andy!"

Sure enough, the big, funny-looking puppy with the black ears was running in circles in the backyard. His long pink tongue was lolling out of his mouth and he was grinning a doggy grin.

"He must have run away," Erin said. "Oh, Daddy, what are we going to do?"

"First, we're going to bring him inside," Doc said. "Then we're going to call the Baumgartners to tell them where he is so they can pick him up."

He headed for the back door with Val, Teddy, Erin, and Sparky close behind. The minute they came outside, Andy dashed up onto the porch and flung himself at Val, barking and trying to lick her face. Jocko zipped between Doc's legs and began frisking around the pup, yelping at the top of his lungs. Somehow everybody stumbled back into the kitchen, all laughing and talking at once.

"Looks like that there pup thinks *this* is his home," Mike said as he joined them. "Guess he wants to spend Thanksgiving with his own folks."

Mrs. Sparks laughed. "He is the *silliest* looking dog . . ."

When Val had managed to calm both Andy and Jocko down, Doc went over to the telephone. "Erin, find Edward Baumgartner in the phone book," he said. "I'm going to call him right away."

"But Daddy, if he ran way from them . . ." Erin started to say, but Doc shook his head.

"He's their dog now, honey. They'll be worried about him."

Slowly but obediently, Erin found the number, and Doc dialed it. It was very quiet in the Taylors' kitchen as he said, "Mr. Baumgartner? This is Doctor Taylor, from Animal Inn. Your dog just turned up in our backyard . . ."

Val held her breath, wondering what Andy's new owner would have to say.

Doc frowned as he listened. "I see. But you must remember that Andy is still very young, and young dogs, like young people, are very high-spirited. . . .

You want to return him to the shelter?"

Erin and Teddy clutched Val's hands. They held onto each other very tightly as Doc said, "Yes, I understand that you've changed your mind. But you don't have to worry about a thing — I'm sure we can find another home for him. . . . Yes, I'll be in touch with you about it tomorrow. And in the meantime, Mr. Baumgartner, happy Thanksgiving!"

He hung up the phone and Mrs. Sparks said, "Ted, do we have one more guest for Thanksgiving dinner?"

"Dad, does that mean we can adopt Andy now?" Val asked.

Doc grinned at Val and Mrs. Sparks. "Yes to both questions. If everybody agrees, that is."

"Yes, yes, yes!" Teddy, Erin and Sparky yelled, jumping up and down.

"Sounds like a good idea to me," Mike muttered as he patted both dogs. "Sounds like you shoulda done it a while ago, Doc."

Doc clapped him on the shoulder. "You know something, Mike? You're right!"

It was after two o'clock by the time the dogs and Cleveland had been fed and everyone was ready to sit down to dinner. Since Cleveland was the only member of the family who wasn't overjoyed by Andy's return, Val had to feed him in her room so he wouldn't have to cope with the pup just yet. Doc had asked Mrs. Sparks to sit at one end of the table, and as she took her place, Erin whispered to Val, "it's nice having Sparky's mother here, isn't it? She made the gravy, and it doesn't have any lumps the way mine always does."

When Doc brought in the golden-brown turkey and set it in front of his place, he said, "Before I start to carve, I think we should all give thanks for the good things in our lives. As for me, I'm thankful that we're all here together, sharing this wonderful feast."

Sparky said, "*I'm* thankful that Teddy hasn't pulled my pigtails even once . . ." She made a face at Teddy. ". . . so far!"

"I'm thankful for being here with all you nice people," Mrs. Sparks said, smiling at everyone. "And thank *you*, Ted, for inviting Philomena and me to be a part of your family celebration."

"I'm glad I still got most of my teeth so I can dig into all this good food," Mike said with a grin.

Then it was Val's turn. Looking around the table at her family and friends, she hesitated a moment before she spoke. "I'm thankful that we had so many Thanksgivings with Sunshine while he was young and strong," she said softly. She glanced into the living room where Jocko and Andy were happily having a tug-of-war with the old rubber pull-toy. "And I'm awfully glad that Andy came home, because this is where he belongs!"

Animals you'll love...
a series you won't want to miss!

ANIMAL INN

by Virginia Vail

Thirteen-year-old Val Taylor looks forward to afternoons every-day! That's when she gets to spend time with a menagerie of horses, dogs, cats, and other animals, great and small. They're all residents at her dad's veterinary clinic, Animal Inn.

Look for these Apple® titles!

❑ MY43434-9	#1	Pets Are for Keeps	$2.75
❑ MY42787-3	#2	A Kid's Best Friend	$2.75
❑ MY43433-0	#3	Monkey Business	$2.75
❑ MY43432-2	#4	Scaredy Cat	$2.75
❑ MY43431-4	#5	Adopt-a-Pet	$2.75
❑ MY43430-6	#6	All the Way Home	$2.75
❑ MY42798-9	#7	The Pet Makeover	$2.75
❑ MY42799-7	#8	Petnapped	$2.75

Available wherever you buy books...
or use the coupon below.

Scholastic Inc. P.O. Box 7502, 2932 E. McCarty Street,
Jefferson City, MO 65102

Please send me the books I have checked above. I am enclosing $__________
(please add $2.00 to cover shipping and handling). Send check or money order—no cash or C.O.D.'s please.

Name ____________________

Address ____________________

City __________ State/Zip __________

Please allow four to six weeks for delivery. Offer good in U.S.A. only.
Sorry, mail order not available to residents of Canada. Prices subject to change.

AI889

by Ann M. Martin

The seven girls at Stoneybrook Middle School get into all kinds of adventures...with school, boys, and, of course, baby-sitting!

❑ NI43388-1	#1	Kristy's Great Idea	$2.95
❑ NI43513-2	#2	Claudia and the Phantom Phone Calls	$2.95
❑ NI43511-6	#3	The Truth About Stacey	$2.95
❑ NI42498-X	#30	Mary Anne and the Great Romance	$2.95
❑ NI42497-1	#31	Dawn's Wicked Stepsister	$2.95
❑ NI42496-3	#32	Kristy and the Secret of Susan	$2.95
❑ NI42495-5	#33	Claudia and the Great Search	$2.95
❑ NI42494-7	#34	Mary Anne and Too Many Boys	$2.95
❑ NI42508-0	#35	Stacey and the Mystery of Stoneybrook	$2.95
❑ NI43565-5	#36	Jessi's Baby-sitter	$2.95
❑ NI43566-3	#37	Dawn and the Older Boy	$2.95
❑ NI43567-1	#38	Kristy's Mystery Admirer	$2.95
❑ NI43568-X	#39	Poor Mallory!	$2.95
❑ NI44082-9	#40	Claudia and the Middle School Mystery	$2.95
❑ NI43570-1	#41	Mary Anne Versus Logan (Feb. '91)	$2.95
❑ NI44083-7	#42	Jessi and the Dance School Phantom (Mar. '91)	$2.95
❑ NI43571-X	#43	Stacey's Revenge (Apr. '91)	$2.95
❑ NI44240-6		Baby-sitters on Board! Super Special #1	$3.50
❑ NI44239-2		Baby-sitters' Summer Vacation Super Special #2	$3.50
❑ NI43973-1		Baby-sitters' Winter Vacation Super Special #3	$3.50
❑ NI42493-9		Baby-sitters' Island Adventure Super Special #4	$3.50
❑ NI43575-2		California Girls! Super Special #5	$3.50

For a complete listing of all the Baby-sitter Club titles write to:
Customer Service at the address below.

Available wherever you buy books...or use this order form.

Scholastic Inc., P.O. Box 7502, 2931 E. McCarty Street, Jefferson City, MO 65102

Please send me the books I have checked above. I am enclosing $ ______________
(please add $2.00 to cover shipping and handling). Send check or money order — no cash or C.O.D.s please.

Name ______________________________

Address ______________________________

City ______________________ State/Zip ______________________

Please allow four to six weeks for delivery. Offer good in U.S.A. only. Sorry, mail orders are not available to residents of Canada. Prices subject to change.

BSC790

Pack your bags for fun and adventure with

- ❑ MF40641-8 #1 Patti's Luck $2.50
- ❑ MF40642-6 #2 Starring Stephanie $2.50
- ❑ MF40643-4 #3 Kate's Surprise $2.50
- ❑ MF40644-2 #4 Patti's New Look $2.50
- ❑ MF41336-8 #5 Lauren's Big Mix-Up $2.50
- ❑ MF41337-6 #6 Kate's Camp-Out $2.50
- ❑ MF41694-4 #7 Stephanie Strikes Back $2.50
- ❑ MF41695-2 #8 Lauren's Treasure $2.50
- ❑ MF41696-0 #9 No More Sleepovers, Patti? $2.50
- ❑ MF41697-9 #10 Lauren's Sleepover Exchange $2.50
- ❑ MF41845-9 #11 Stephanie's Family Secret $2.50
- ❑ MF41846-7 #12 Kate's Sleepover Disaster $2.50
- ❑ MF42301-0 #13 Patti's Secret Wish $2.50
- ❑ MF42300-2 #14 Lauren Takes Charge $2.50
- ❑ MF42299-5 #15 Stephanie's Big Story $2.50
- ❑ MF42662-1 Sleepover Friends' Super Guide $2.50
- ❑ MF42366-5 #16 Kate's Crush $2.50
- ❑ MF42367-3 #17 Patti Gets Even $2.50
- ❑ MF42814-4 #18 Stephanie and the Magician $2.50
- ❑ MF42815-2 #19 The Great Kate $2.50
- ❑ MF42816-0 #20 Lauren in the Middle $2.50
- ❑ MF42817-9 #21 Starstruck Stephanie $2.50
- ❑ MF42818-7 #22 The Trouble with Patti $2.50
- ❑ MF42819-5 #23 Kate's Surprise Visitor $2.50
- ❑ MF43194-3 #24 Lauren's New Friend $2.50

Available wherever you buy books...or use the coupon below.

Scholastic Inc. P.O. Box 7502, 2932 E. McCarty Street, Jefferson City, MO 65102

Please send me the books I have checked above. I am enclosing $__________

(Please add $2.00 to cover shipping and handling). Send check or money order–no cash or C.O.D. s please

Name ____________________

Address ____________________

City __________ State/Zip __________

Please allow four to six weeks for delivery. Offer good in U.S.A. only. Sorry, mail orders are not available to residents of Canada. Prices subject to change.

SLE1089